SING

LOVE STORIES

SINGAPORE
LOVE STORIES

VERENA TAY
(EDITOR)

monsoon

monsoonbooks

First published in 2016
by Monsoon Books Ltd
www.monsoonbooks.com.sg

No.1 Duke of Windsor Suite, Burrough Court,
Burrough on the Hill, Leics. LE14 2QS, UK
and 150 Orchard Road #07-02, Singapore 238841.

First edition.

ISBN (paperback): 978-981-4625-49-4
ISBN (ebook): 978-981-4625-50-0

Cataloguing in Publication Data: a catalogue record for this book
is available from the National Library, Singapore.

Published with the support of

NATIONAL ARTS COUNCIL
SINGAPORE

Printed in Great Britain by Clays Ltd, St Ives plc
18 17 16   1 2 3 4 5

MIX
Paper from
responsible sources
FSC® C018072

CONTENTS

ACKNOWLEDGEMENTS

The following contributors, Damyanti Biswas, Audrey Chin, Marion Kleinschmidt, S. Mickey Lin and Shola Olowu-Asante, were instrumental in helping *Singapore Love Stories* move beyond ideation to a fully-fledged project.

Many thanks go to Verena Tay for agreeing to take on such a large project with a diverse team of writers. Verena has facilitated a story collection that tackles the theme of love in ways that are universal and yet recognisably local. Her impeccable knowledge of Singapore's geography and of its cultural and linguistic nuances kept minor inaccuracies from creeping into the manuscript. She generously edited and worked with the contributors to ensure their vision of love soars on the page.

I want to thank each of the contributors for believing that there are always new love stories to be told. Against the backdrop of the Lion City, they have each created a unique narrative that challenges set notions of what a love story can be.

Some authors within these pages explore: grief, duplicity and revenge, self-love, filial love, homesickness and tragic past relationships. Others have taken their pieces to speculative and magical heights, reminding us that falling in love is a leap into new territories. Collectively, the stories in this anthology reveal the many ways in which love can be both a salve and a wound in our lives.

This book would not exist were it not for the people

mentioned above and for Philip Tatham at Monsoon Books, whose enthusiasm and belief in both the writers and the vision made *Singapore Love Stories* an actuality.

Raelee Chapman
Anthology Coordinator & Compiler

INTRODUCTION

Although love is a universal human attribute, its manifestations within human beings are complex and contradictory. Not only are there many kinds of love (e.g. familial, heterosexual, homosexual or comradely affections; self-esteem; passions for certain objects or pursuits), but the nature of love is also very much influenced by socio-economic and political considerations.

So what does it mean to love and be loved in Singapore with its fluid yet diverse population and particular social constraints? The book in your hands attempts to answer this question.

The short stories within this anthology are written by a variety of writers residing or formerly residing in Singapore. Each story features a unique protagonist who confronts his/her attitudes towards other characters whom they hold dear amidst everyday challenges of living within the Lion City.

Collectively, the stories bring to life a vivid cross-section of Singapore society: from the HDB heartlander to the Sentosa millionaire, from the privileged expatriate to the lowly imported contract worker, from the accidental tourist to the reluctant citizen, from the dedicated artisan to the sly con-artist. While the anthology does not claim to possess a definitive view about love in Singapore, it does reveal an array of perspectives that intrigue, touch the heart and give pause for thought and wonder.

Whether you are an armchair traveller or someone at home on the Little Red Dot reading *Singapore Love Stories*, we wish you an insightful and inspiring journey. Enjoy!

Verena Tay
Editor & Contributing Writer

A POOR MAN

AUDREY CHIN

Anna, older brother! Please be accepting my abject apologies that you are firstly hearing about my affairs from *anna mukavar*, our fellow villager, and not myself. Also please be accepting my apologies that this letter is in English. But, you must also be agreeing, these are not matters our family should be worrying about.

To start, I must say I am still not quite sure how this has happened to me. As you are asking however, let me try to explain.

In the beginning, I am not thinking anything about marrying. That time, I am lately arrived in Singapore. I am still paying off agents' fees and tickets and many etcetera like my safety kit and working shoes and the deposit for my bunk in quarters. Like you tell me, I am a youngest son, a poor man; nobody will marry a poor man. So ... the matter is entirely out from my mind.

Then, one Saturday I am fainting on the roadside and waking to see the fat lady's servant, Melli-ann, holding a yellow umbrella over my head ...

I am falling where we are doing drainage works in Sunset Way. We are working here the last fourteen days, in a tunnel next to the fat lady's house. That time it is the hot season and no wind is blowing in and no wind is going out of our workplace. All day long we breathe only steam from stagnant water and stink from rotting leaves. It is like being dead and being burnt over a river. Fourteen days I am trying to bear it, thinking ahead what to do with the hard-time money I will be getting, telling myself I am strong. But it is no good. Saturday clock-out, I climb out from the *longkang* ready to enjoy my off-time like a man. But what is happening? I find myself lying on the cement floor with a goddess looking down at me.

This goddess is surrounded by yellow umbrella light and has eyes soft like Coimbatore velvet and wet like our father's favourite milk-cow. This is causing me much confusion, like something is cracking in my head and my heart. For some small time I am not knowing if I am gone back home to our father's farm or arrived in heaven. But then I am realising this goddess is only the maid belonging to the fat lady, the Ma'am who sends ice-water out for us at break-times and clock-out every day. Like the fat lady, she is kind. When I am falling down, *mukavar* tells me later, she is the one calling for her Ma'am. She is the one putting the ice-water towel on my head. She is the one who informs me, fat lady is allowing me to come into the air-conditioning house to recover.

"You have a good owner," I am telling this servant.

Her face turns to ice. "She is not my owner. She is my employer and I am her employee," she tells me very slow and loud like I am stupid. Then she rolls her eyes at me and turns away. When I am better to go outside, she is talking only with *mukavar*, never bothers with me again, even I am younger and more handsome.

After that time, I am always watching Melli-ann. I am not straight staring like some country idiot, but just before I give her the water cup back I will steal one look. I also tell her to thank the fat lady. "Your employer," I remember to use that word. Melli-ann, she is never answering. She pretends she has forgotten the first time we talk. But I see that she smiles.

Anna mukavar, he is also seeing.

Before, he already warned me: Filipinas, they only look up; if I want I must go for a Sri Lankan or Indonesian. Now he is showing me his small finger and twisting it around like winding cotton. "Be careful. When a Filipina looks at you, this is what they will be doing. Before you know, you will be sending all your saving to her family farm. You will see."

"She is kind. She is having nice teeth," I answer him. "And this also …" I make the number eight with my hands, two curves on top, two curves lower.

"Cheaper you pay $10 for short time in Serangoon. You go with one like her, you will have nothing to take home for a house, nothing for your marriage."

He is older and wiser. But still, I am daring to answer him. "I can dream, no? And if I am also wanting the other thing and can get free, it is $10 to save. Why not?"

He tells me back, "And when have I seen her talking to you?"

I smile. "You wait and see."

It is come up to the rainy season and still I am waiting. But I am not despairing. We are finished digging. Now we are laying pipe outside. I am breathing fresh air. Also, I am three months senior now, experienced enough to take watchman duty. That is one-and-a-half time pay to sleep overnight by the tool shed. No more crowding twelve men to one room in quarters, no more sharing everybody's wet dreaming and nightmaring. What more, I am having spare to send a bigger remittance home.

"Your life is being good now, yes?" *mukavar* says when handing me my dinner-money.

He is right. Almost. I point to my sleeping tent. "I am only needing one thing more – a Filipina under this rubber sheet with me," I reply.

Anna mukavar, he pats my hand. "It's end of the year school holiday."

"Huh?"

He is smiling like a man sharing a stolen honeypot. But I am not understanding.

"Holiday time, bosses all going away with their children. Maids are free," he tells me. He tilts his head towards the resting pavilion in the middle of the park. "Your honey chicken is there. Also friends. Next two weeks, every night they will be there. All hungry hens, eating and talking. Best time for you to be taking a chance." He hands me an extra $10. "Take. I score a free Sri Lankan last weekend," he is saying. Moreover he is advising me, "Go to the food court and buy some food to share with them. You can pay back my money next day, after you also score."

I am not paying *anna mukavar* back the next day. What I offer to Melli-ann – twelve hot chicken wings from the food court at the starting of Sunset Way – is giving me just one seat in the pavilion and, afterwards, one invitation to come again. I am having to invest much more in Jollibee, Pizza Hut and light beer for many more nights before I score one. This, I must explain, is why my remittance home is late last time.

Also, I must report, I am not scoring with Melli-ann. Like *mukavar* says, there are many coming and going to that place. Those ones, they are happy hearing me tell about Ullikottai and reasoning why I am here. They are also listening to my planning for a house and my future wife. Some are informing me that Filipino men are not so careful like me. They are admiring I am not letting my future wife work, not sending her away to Saudi or Singapore to be a servant like their husbands. I am having an appreciating audience. Mostly. Except for Melli-ann.

When I talk, Melli-ann is mostly rolling her eyes. And, when I am finished and the girls are playing guitar and singing, she is telling me why she is not impressed.

"What for you want to go home and be a farmer? So boring on a farm. Better to stay here until they kick you out," she is scolding me. "You never think! $100 there, $1000 here for the same work," she is making it her business to tell me. As if we Indians cannot count better than Filipinas!

"I'm knowing that," I reply to her. "But this is not my home."

"Without money, home is just people fighting and fucking and beating each other up. It's nothing to talk about."

"At home everyone is being together. No matter what, still all the same blood."

"Tchhhhhh!" she is baring her teeth at me. They are curving like a sickle, cutting across her face. "Don't talk to me about same blood together! Father and daughter, brother and sister, what do you know about it?" she is spitting out.

Obviously, I am upsetting her upside down and up again, but for what I am not clear.

No, I may be wanting, but it cannot be Melli-ann that I am scoring with.

I am scoring with Christalle. This one has short curling hair and likes to be called Billy. She is always teasing that my eyelashes are sooooo long and soooo pretty I should be a girl. Sometimes I want to tell her she should be a man because she is joking too far for a girl. But I am not doing that. Anyway, she is the one who is opening my tent-flap and pushing herself in late on Christmas night. "I have a present for you … And for me … " she is saying. And then she is reaching under my *lungi*.

I am not wanting to be a pretty boy Christmas present for some she-he. But Billy, she has a body like a wrestler. I will not be winning if I fight her. And certainly, my small tent will be falling down if we are moving too much. I am thinking it is a December thunderstorm outside. I am not wanting to be soaking wet, I am also thinking. My third leg, it does not do so much thinking. Before I can even count how many fingers Billy is using on it, I must confess to you, I am already boiling over like a pot of *pongal* rice.

After this I am having different ideas about Melli-ann's friends. Sure, nobody is as beautiful as Melli-ann with her soft eyes and her breasts like young coconuts. Nobody is giving me better advice for taking care of myself. But Billy, she can sing like a professional; any kind of American song, any style. And she is very expert with her holding here and there. When she is wrestling with me, I am not caring who ends on top or underneath. Whether she is pressing me down or turning me over, this Billy is sending me flying.

There is also Mie Mie from Burma … This one is never saying a word in the pavilion. She is like a puppet – flat chest, skinny arms, thin legs and nodding head. But she has a thick plait that is long to her hipbones and blacker than midnight. She is pinning it up when she works. At night though, she lets it run free down her back. And I am noticing that every time she is shifting her head, this plait is twisting and slapping like a panther's tail. Maybe, I am guessing, she is not just a wooden doll …

Like our father is telling us from young, even a broken pot can contain sugar. I am looking at Melli-ann all the time for honey and starving when anytime I can be eating sweetmeats at her neighbours!

In the New Year, I am able to give *anna mukavar* back $40 for his $10. But, *mukavar* is not accepting it. "I am not one who is here, there and also taking a share of the boiled rice," he says. "First you are looking at the oldest sister. Now you get the younger one and also you are playing with the cousin. You know what happens to a man's top-knot when he has two wives?"

"He will lose it when they fight," I reply. "But I don't have a top-knot. And these two, they are not my wives. Also, you know how they live working in those houses. It is worse than being a widow. I am giving them something to dream about during working time. No one will be tearing my hair out because of that."

Anna mukavar rolls his eyes, same way like Melli-ann. "If you want to try different cooking, don't go to next-door shops," he says. "Also you want to know who is your number one before you are losing it doing something stupid. Think about that."

"Who is my number one?" I am knowing the answer to this question, but I am not knowing how to make this answer happen. Anyway, New Year is over and also my night-watch. The Ma'ams have all come home. We have no more gatherings in the pavilion. I have no more chance to wrestle with Billy or play with Mie Mie's plait. Melli-ann is not having anything to get angry about. I am not even saying enough for her to roll her eyes or scold me.

Only we are saying "have a drink" and "please" and "tell your employer I am thanking her" and "don't mention" and "you are welcome".

"I miss you," she is also saying one evening at clock-out.

"I'm missing all of you too," I say.

She rolls her eyes. "All of us?" she asks.

I look down, shuffling my feet.

And then she is saying, "My ma'am is watching fireworks this weekend. You want to come eat with me?"

I am sometimes so practical I become stupid. "Lorry comes at 6.30. I cannot miss it. Otherwise, I am paying $10 for taxi back to quarters or sleeping on the roadside," I reply.

Melli-ann turns away. Her face is part angry, part something else, same way like our cow when we take away her baby to sell. "As you like," she says.

I can be saying, "No, I don't like but that is life for a poor man." Maybe she can be forgiving me then. But what I am actually doing is walking to the lorry and jumping onto it and watching like a fool as Melli-Ann walks away and the fat lady's gate closes.

If I am writing you a story, older brother, this will be the end. That night in quarters, *mukavar* tells us we are changing assignment the next day. Next morning, we will be working on connection pipes at the main road. This is 700 metres from the fat lady's house. I have no chance to see Melli-ann again, don't be talking about saying sorry or anything like that.

But this is not a story. It is real life. *Anna mukavar* is our fellow villager and he is looking out for me. The next day, he asks us to take tea-break in the Sunset Way food court. And before we are drinking, he is saying loudly to all of us, "I am missing some tools and gloves. I am thinking they are left at yesterday's site. Who wants to go back to check?" It is burning hot. He is knowing well nobody is wanting to walk all the way back to the fat lady's except one of us. He looks straight at this very one. This time, I am not slow to understand. Before he is saying my name, I am already racing out the food court and into the estate.

Every day at tea-break, the fat lady is opening her gate and leaving to pick up her grandchildren from school. At this time, Melli-ann is coming out with our water. Today we are not there. There is no open gate and no Melli-ann. But I have run all the way down Sunset Way to here in less than four minutes. I cannot lose hope. I look through the wood strips on the gate, hoping the fat lady is still gone for her grandchildren ...

I am lucky. The garage is empty!

I press the bell. There is ringing inside the house. Then the speaker on the gate-post clicks.

"Why are you here?" Melli-ann is asking.

"I want to talk to you," I answer.

Melli-ann's voice comes back. "I don't talk to stupid people."

"I want to say I am sorry I am making you angry," I tell her.

"Who says I am angry? I have no reason to be angry. You are nothing to me. How can you make me angry?" she asks, her talking fast and loud.

Of course she is angry. But I will be making her angrier if I say. So, I keep my mouth shut and chew on my tongue.

The speaker clicks off.

I almost give up. But I cannot be going back to *anna mukavar* empty-handed after all his help. And certainly I myself will be regretting forever if I surrender so easily ... I ring the doorbell again.

"I am a man. I cannot let you be getting away from my life like this," I shout into the speaker.

The speaker is staying quiet.

I ring the doorbell one more time. "I am wanting you to know you are the most beautiful woman to me," I say.

Still nothing.

"I am wanting to say I love you," I say next. I am adding, "I am wanting to ask you to marry me."

There is nothing better I can be offering. I wait.

The gate begins to open.

"What is it? Is there a problem?" The fat lady's voice is coming into my ear. She is leaning out of her car window, the gate opener in her hand.

"Aa-iii, ah, my boss he wants me to tell you we are moved. He says he is grateful for your water," I reply.

"It's nothing," the fat lady waves away my words. Then she is winding up her window and driving into the driveway and her gate is closing again.

Behind the gate, I can hear the grandchildren calling for Melli-ann. But Melli-ann is still at the speaker. I can hear her sigh one in and then one out.

"Are you hearing me?" I ask her.

"Sunday afternoon, three o'clock, at the food court," she replies. And then the speaker clicks off and she is shouting in the garden, "Sorry Ma'am! I'm coming!"

I am early at the food court on Sunday, too early. When Melli-ann comes down the road, her whole person shining under her yellow umbrella, I am already nearly finishing my fourth

Guinness. Maybe, this is why I am not clearly thinking when she arrives to stand in front of me, snaps her umbrella shut and shouts at me, "You fresh-off-the-boats, you're all the same. This is why I never encouraged you! I knew you'd end up being this stupid! This possessive!"

How can it be stupid to fall in love? To ask the woman you love to marry you? I am not saying all this but I must be looking these questions because Melli-ann, she is answering. She is scolding, "Don't you know the situation we're in? We come, and if our bosses don't like, we go, not even one day's notice. How can we promise anybody anything? Marriage! Only idiots can believe they're rich enough to want it." And then she bumps onto the bench next to me and sighs.

"We can pretend," I am managing to interrupt before she can start scolding again.

She looks at me. And now her brown eyes are soft and wet again. "I have a husband in the Philippines. And one son. What can you pretend about that?"

This I am not expecting. But I am strengthened by nearly four Guinness. I am not going backwards. "They are not here. We do not have to be pretending anything about them," I tell her. I slip one foot from my sandal and rub them over her toes. "I am here."

She rubs my toes back with her other foot. We sit like this, side by side, playing with our feet and taking sips from my last bottle for a long time. All the while, I am feeling hotter and hotter. "Let us be going somewhere," I say to her finally.

She swish-swishes the last mouthful of Guinness in her mouth and swallows. "What about Billy and Mie Mie," she asks.

This Melli-ann, she wants to care for everybody, give

27

everybody water even when she is not having any! And why not, I ask myself.

"I am a poor man but there is enough of me to share if you are willing," I say to her, my number one.

But, it seems I am doing something wrong again! Melli-ann is drawing her body away from me. "Tchhh ..." she is almost exploding. And then, she is changing her mind.

"Something is better than nothing, I suppose," she is muttering. "If you can pretend I am not married, then ..."

She sighs. I can feel her hand searching. Then, she is hooking her smallest finger around mine.

So my *anna*, this is how I am become like a landlord, three women to my name rotating through my off-days. It is completely out of my mind. But do not be worrying. I am knowing my responsibilities. *Mukavar* is giving me much night-watch duty. Your remittances will be arriving as usually. As I said earlier to explain why I am writing in English, it is not needed to distress our father with these matters.

About the Author
Audrey Chin is a cartographer of the heart. Her fiction includes *Nine Cuts*, a short story collection (Math Paper Press, May 2015) and two novels – *As the Heart Bones Break* (2013) and *Learning to Fly* (1999) – all of which have been shortlisted for the Singapore Literature Prize.

She is also contributing co-editor of *Singapore Women Re-presented* (2004), a social history of Singapore. She has been published by Cobalt Review, the Rand Corporation, the Singapore Council of Women's Organisations and World Scientific. In

November 2015 she came out as a praying woman with the prayer book, *When Heart Meets Spirit*.

SAGO LANE

HEATHER HIGGINS

"Argh argh argh." The sounds that Grandmother made were half gargle and half gagging throat. It caused Charlotte's mother to leave the room, retching. Charlotte herself had to press her hand to her mouth, but she stayed, putting her other hand on Grandmother's thin shoulder and gently rubbing until the woman went quiet.

Sometimes her wretched sounds became a kind of babble, almost-words the old woman repeated over and over, looking intensely at all the family at dinner, while their eyes glazed over and their smiles froze on their faces.

There were rare moments when her words made sense as if her brain had suddenly switched on. Looking at Charlotte with frightened eyes, she asked, "Where am I?" But she was gone before the answer was out of Charlotte's mouth. Then the teenager pulled her chair close to her grandmother's and held her crabbed hand, trying to show the old woman that she understood.

Over time, as the old woman's attempts to speak became less frequent, she grew restless, as if there was some place important for her to go to. She wandered the flat at all hours, shuffling along between the arms of her walker. Sometimes they even found her at the door, one hand gripping the walker, while the other fumbled with the locks and her wretched noises bounced off the walls of the tiny entry.

It was not long before she got herself out of the flat and all the way to the lift, while the maid worked on, oblivious.

"How did she do it?" Charlotte heard her mother cry after they had gotten the elderly woman back inside and in front of the TV. "She can't even feed herself, but she can get out of the place?"

All Charlotte wondered about was where her grandmother wanted to go.

"How many times do I have to tell you? Grandmother is senile. She doesn't know where she is, much less where she is going." Her mother pointed to her own head, her face a knot of anger and sadness.

Charlotte remembered when her grandmother knew everything there was to know. When she pulled the leaves of a pandan plant by the school fence and explained how to use it to flavour a dish. Or whispered the names of the kampongs and villages that used to lie along the route their bus passed. She spoke of the large funeral processions that passed Chinatown's streets when she was a child, the special clothes the mourners wore, the way the men walked, then knelt, then waved their joss sticks up and down as the women wailed, how the incense hung heavy in the air after the procession passed.

As Charlotte grew older, the tales were forgotten. Grandmother increasingly needed her to count out the money at the wet market or remind her which bus to board and where to alight. She went around the kitchen, touching the bowls and spoons and putting her hand on the wok as if she might use it, but she was afraid to turn the heat on now. So Charlotte followed behind her, talking about school and friends while she selected the spices her grandmother forgot, put away the things the old woman pulled out, and made the meal while pretending her grandmother did it all.

Charlotte had learned about metaphors in English, but it was only when she found herself doing all the cooking for her grandmother that she realised such things had meaning in life too.

Now when her mother came home from the office and found her daughter preparing food for the family, she got angry. "Ay yi, you are cooking too much! What about your O-Levels? You must study!"

But Grandmother would not eat the food from the hawker centre. She ate nothing prepared by the maid either, swatting the young woman's hand viciously.

Finally, Charlotte's mother accepted that her daughter did the cooking, but only in so far as it did not affect her marks. So they resumed their afternoon ritual, Charlotte chatting to Grandmother while preparing the food, asking questions and answering them as if the old woman were still all there.

Some nights, when Charlotte studied particularly late, when she could not look at any more books, nor memorise any more equations, she tiptoed down the hall to her grandmother's room and stood outside the door. She heard the old woman's harsh breathing and the coughing that rattled up out of her chest. And Charlotte wondered yet again, where Grandmother wanted to go so badly.

One day on a whim, Charlotte went to the library and took out a book about old Singapore, containing pages and pages of black and white photographs from her grandmother's time and before. She carried the book home cradled in her arms and put it in her grandmother's lap.

The elderly woman did not even notice it. And when Charlotte came home after school, she found that the maid had tidied the book out of reach. The girl insisted to the maid, "When you move my grandmother, put the book nearby. Open it on a page, any page, and leave it there." The days went by, and though the book was often in Grandmother's lap, the pictures seemed to mean nothing to her.

Until one day, when she came home exhausted after her last exam, Charlotte found Grandmother bent over in her chair sputtering and gagging and pounding her finger on the book. She hit it over and over until Charlotte slipped it out from under her hands and she became silent.

That evening, when her mother returned from work, Charlotte brought the book to her and showed her the page that had caused her grandmother such excitement.

Her mother looked at it for a minute or so. "Well, I guess we know what Grandmother wants," she said, straightening her shoulders and looking ahead of her, not seeing anything.

Later, Charlotte opened the book again to the same page. The photos were old, a little out of focus. One showed a rough-looking shophouse, Chinese characters written down each pillar. The other was an interior shot, all murky and grey. In its grim shadows, Charlotte could make out figures lying on platforms and, standing to one side, an attendant dressed in pyjamas, looking at the camera.

A paragraph described how Sago Lane was once lined with funeral parlours, with death houses above them, where the poor came to die with no food and only a little water to wet the lips, if the family paid the attendant.

The next morning after Mother and Father went to work, Charlotte went into Grandmother's room and woke her. She gently pulled the old woman up to sitting and wiped her limbs with a damp cloth. She slid a fresh clean top over the wrinkled arms, tugged elastic-waisted pants up the thin legs to her tiny waist. She was so light now, it was no effort to lift her into the wheelchair.

The taxi driver left them on South Bridge Road under the sign for Sago Lane. After settling her grandmother in the wheelchair, Charlotte straightened up and looked around. To her left, there was a half-empty car park with tour buses parked along its perimeter. In front of her rose the Chinatown Complex and to her right, the more recently built Buddha Tooth Relic Temple, its maroon-coloured walls smooth and unmarked by time.

Pushing the chair along the lane around to the back of the temple, she was afraid for a moment that she might come upon those old death houses, with their grim inhabitants laid out on platforms. But there were no funeral parlours with death houses above, nor shops selling funerary goods in the lane behind the temple. All she saw were a few cleaned-up shophouses with food stalls out front, and the Singapore Tourist Office standing guard, with its shiny glass walls and neat stand of brochures just to the left of the door.

It struck Charlotte that all this time she'd been expecting her grandmother to improve. With the good food she was making and the tender care, she'd believed that one day the old woman would look up at her and converse for real. That she would take over again in the kitchen and make with her own hands the dishes the family loved.

But now she knew that her grandmother would soon be gone. Charlotte would take her home and they would probably never go out of the flat together again. Soon the old woman would no longer leave her bed. Then there would be nothing more Charlotte could do for her except daub her skin with a damp cloth and wet her lips with water, while the old woman drifted away on memories of things that were no longer there.

When she reached the front of the temple with the wheelchair, Charlotte peered through the large doors. A family stood before a statue of Buddha. As the father helped his little girl select joss sticks from the box, the mother began to pray, bending forward repeatedly to the Buddha. The woman held her joss sticks high above her head and waved them up and down, tossing the fragrant smoke into the air, where it was caught by the powerful fans and quickly blown away.

About the Author

Heather Higgins was born in New York City, received her degree in Renaissance Studies from Barnard College, Columbia University, and worked as an advertising copywriter and creative director for twenty years. Since arriving in Singapore in 2008, she has been a docent and trainer in the Singapore Art Museum, volunteered at her twins' school and written two unpublished novels and a couple dozen stories. "Sago Lane" is her first published fiction piece. Heather is a Singapore Permanent Resident.

LOVE, NUDE

ELAINE CHIEW

All week Teck Hin has been tossing about in his mind how to ask
this of Yee Lan: *will you pose for me?* He wants to draw her. In
charcoal on paper. Paint her. Gouache on ink paper. A silhouette
of her. Front. Back. A multitude of sketches.

But nude. Totally, baldly nude.

Yee Lan is Aunty Boon Leng's sixteen-year-old daughter – as
seemingly fragile as rice paper, her hair an unbroken line of black
threads, her expression as serene and graceful as the Goddess Kuan
Yin. Which is why Teck Hin, who is studying at the Nan Fang Fine
Arts Academy, wants to draw her. The idea of a figurative drawing
with Chinese characteristics and yet hydraulically sucking on the
teat of Western art tradition of the female nude appeals to him (as
transgressive as Manet's Olympia, as sexually explicit as Schiele,
as blending of East/West as Utamaru). This year is his break-out
year. One can't imbibe or endure all that Marxist or feminist
deconstructionist art criticism without wanting to demolish
accepted cultural iconography and yield to primeval tendencies.
His mentor at school, an iconoclast and rebel himself who had
idolised the Nanyang-style artist Cheng Soo Pieng, wants to
channel that spirit and tells him that his chances of winning one
of the country's top prizes for young emerging artists are good,

but he needs to submit something self-defining, and even better, something that will shake up the Singaporean art world.

But the problem is two-fold. Yee Lan will probably be hesitant, if not refuse him outright – he can already see the blush creeping up her neck and face. He knows he's utilising the fact that she has feelings for him, has had them since primary school, which will make it difficult for her to refuse. She has a weak heart, metaphorically and literally; in Primary 5, she'd collapsed due to arrhythmia when he was taking her to buy cut guava at a food court. Luckily, there was a hospital two blocks away, and Teck Hin had hauled her onto his back and rushed her to Emergency. In return, Yee Lan told him solemnly that she would be a good Christian and pray for him for the rest of her life.

The other part of the problem is Yee Lan's mother. Aunty Boon Leng believes in Teck Hin's talent while nobody in his family does. *Oh, he's going to be famous artist someday, is it not? Look, so gifted. Can draw those attap houses and mangrove swamps like nobody's business.* Aunty Boon Leng constantly remarks on the gratitude she feels because he saved Yee Lan's life, to the point of cloyingness. Though not a real aunt but a friend of her mother's, Aunty Boon Leng dotes on him. *You like my own son, noble and so cool leh?* Asking Yee Lan to pose nude will dispel this magnified image of super-realism she has of him.

He is conflicted, in conscience and feelings; the urge to draw Yee Lan comes upon him heedlessly; he finds himself stealing glances at her soft, plump arms when she wears a T-shirt, or at her pale thighs when she wears shorts. He examines her toes minutely, the way the little toe curves inward and curves more than the others. He memorises her face, her almond-shaped eyes, her smooth cheek-line, the one tiny brown freckle right underneath her left eye in an otherwise unblemished face. Yee Lan blushes like a fiery bride when she catches him looking at her so intently. Acting coquettish, batting her eyelashes, smoothing her skirt, crossing and uncrossing her ankles, a virgin ingénue. Her mannerisms are so incongruous with her posture and mode of dress that she appears all the more adorable to him, like a sister; all the more enticing in that it makes him tingle for wanting to draw her. A vicious circle.

Sitting on the grass at her house after breakfast one Saturday morning, he begins in stealth. Broad pencil strokes to capture the outline of her in a white blouse and demure parachute skirt, her hair neatly plaited on both sides, playing with Dunia, her Scottish terrier, who means the world to her. He leaves her face a blank oval; he will fill that in last. Dunia he captures with all the dexterity he can muster, its limpid eyes, its furry face, its tiny protruding tongue.

"What are you doing?" she asks.

Teck Hin does not reply, intent on drawing.

"Are you drawing me?"

"Why would I draw you?"

"Don't you want to draw me?"

A question so pointed can hardly be avoided, indeed it's the perfect moment to broach the question, yet Teck Hin finds himself overtaken by a perverse impulse. "Are you worthy to be drawn? Modigliani's nudes often sell for hundreds of millions."

"Oh, I wouldn't ever show my body. That's disgraceful." But in the act of rearranging her skirt, Yee Lan pulls the hem higher, revealing her rounded, peachy knees.

Teck Hin smiles to himself. They spend another hour in the shade of the garden's large banyan, and then it is too hot to sit outside.

* * *

Teck Hin draws Yee Lan surreptitiously, ubiquitously, multitudinously. Soon enough, he's produced multiple sketches of Yee Lan. A myriad of charcoal outlines. Yee Lan on a bench, tilting her face up to the sun. Yee Lan peering from behind a Chinese fan (imagined). Yee Lan at the piano, her back ramrod straight, her fingers captured forever in sprightly action. Yee Lan cupping her hands at a water fountain. Yee Lan with Dunia, many of these in various guises and activities. From these sketches, he tries to paint her at the school studio. In watercolour. In pastel. In oils. But for whatever reason, the paintings fail to satisfy. They seem to lack an intrinsic essence of Yee Lan. He tries to imagine her without clothes on. Tries to draw an outline of this, but again, fails.

But what if? If he can't draw Yee Lan nude, could he perhaps superimpose her face on another nude? Would that be dishonest? Didn't artists in collectives substitute one naked body for another, so that the final nude you saw was not one person but actually a composite of perfect limbs and anatomical magnificence? It's a thought, so.

* * *

Aunty Boon Leng considers herself his godmother because she single-handedly persuaded his mother, a High Court Judge, to allow Teck Hin to switch from Law to Art. The two families are so close they could be related, living as they do next door to each other. The mothers attend spa treatments together; the fathers play golf. Teck Hin spent his entire childhood going in and out of Aunty Boon Leng's house whenever he wanted. Even now, he sometimes spends more time at her house than his own, because Aunty Boon Leng cooks like a dream while his mother is never home. Secretly, he knows she cherishes the thought that one day Teck Hin might marry Yee Lan, even though Yee Lan's bad heart makes her defective in other people's eyes, certainly in the eyes of his parents. Teck Hin feels duplicitous, this betrayal on the part of his mother; though admittedly so close, his mother does not wish for Teck Hin to marry Yee Lan because of her health. *Why should you be saddled with looking after her? You have a promising career in front of you.* There are a number of illusions his mother still harbours; for example, his art obsession is just a phase. Eventually, he will come to his senses, go back to Law, find himself a proper sustaining career. Aunty Boon Leng speaks up for him. *He's going to be the Singaporean Jeff Koons.*

As for marrying Yee Lan one day, Teck Hin sometimes thinks about it. Would it be wrong if he doesn't love her?

* * *

Yee Lan discovers the stash of secret drawings. Not entirely secret, because Teck Hin hopes for her to find them. He leaves the sketches lying on top of his satchel haphazardly, excusing himself to go downstairs to bring up a glass of milk and some biscuits for them both.

When he enters the bedroom, Yee Lan's eyes are round with wonder. He pretends to be embarrassed, putting the tray down hurriedly, snatching the drawing pad away. She snatches it back. Gazing at the sketches, she has the look of someone encountering a mystery. It reminds Teck Hin of the painting by Gérôme, of Pygmalion and Galatea. Truly, Yee Lan has never looked as glowingly beautiful and delicate as she does now. The mirror effect is not lost on Teck Hin: we do not know ourselves until we see ourselves reflected in the eyes of our beloved.

"I didn't know you felt this way." A film of moisture now dances and flickers in her eyes. The emotions surging within her are making her chest rise and fall in rapid succession, her cheeks subsumed with rosiness. He feels a quickening, it is now or never. But wait, is she, is she thinking that ...

He says, "I want to ..."

She looks up. Oh, that tilt of chin and elongation of neck. Teck Hin moves swiftly to sit beside her. He covers her hand with his. *What if?* His face draws close, his lips even closer, his breath feathering the epidermis of her upper lip. Yee Lan's breathing goes into overdrive, her nostrils flaring slightly, her lips parting, her eyes darting to his and then looking down. Yes, she has misunderstood. For a second, Teck Hin is struck by the Damocles' sword of what he's doing. Is this the artist playing God, the master puppeteer? If he kisses her, Yee Lan will say yes to anything. And then what? Is he really willing to fabricate reality in order to get what he wants? But isn't that what art is: fabricated reality? Two-dimensional illusions that attempt to impart another reality – of substance and depth, light and colour – when in fact all you are playing with is just surface?

Teck Hin draws back. The spell breaks. Yee Lan flushes violently and bows her head. As if in shame. As if he'd gone ahead and asked her to strip.

* * *

But the deception has begun, despite his ambivalence. Love notes arrive in his email box every morning, love emojis on his cell phone, pressed dried flowers and Milo single-serving milk cartons left on top of his satchel when he takes bathroom breaks. Her eyes full of hope and expectation. Her tentative touches of his wrist and knee. Her giggles. Her batting eyelashes. The full arsenal of female biological behaviour when trying to catch a mate. The change is not lost on Aunty Boon Leng either. If she wasn't already enamoured of him before, now she practically showers gold-dust in the wake of his footsteps.

He feels rotten and undeserving. He does not love Yee Lan. He does not even remotely have a crush. It's strictly an aesthetic need to capture something as elusive as her beauty and purity. The same feeling that explodes in him when he sees a magnificent sunrise, hears a chorus of birds trilling on the branches of trees, sing-songing, serenading each other in the language of bird-love. A sense of being. There's a German word for it: *kunstwollen*. Riegl's word for man's desire to express his relationship with the perceptible appearance of things. In short, Teck Hin's own interpretation and rendering of beauty. No one else's gaze, his own.

Yee Lan wilts under the weight of her own daily expectations, the waiting, the second-guessing of when Teck Hin will make a move. This pains him: seeing those eyes full of limpid hope and desire turning into self-doubt, taking on an expression of desperate longing, searching his face for a glimpse of reciprocal feeling. He tosses about in bed, losing sleep, unwilling to disabuse her of the notion that he likes her, yet unable to move forward to ask her to pose for him.

Inevitably, the sword drops. Yee Lan corners him when he arrives one afternoon, satchel slung across his chest, leaning his bicycle against the wall. "Mother isn't home," she begins, already flustered.

Teck Hin pauses in the middle of unbuckling his helmet. "Oh?"

"Come in quickly. We don't have much time."

"To do what?"

But Yee Lan has already gone indoors to her bedroom.

When he enters, he sees that she is standing behind a screen. The screen is Japanese and obfuscates but little. His heart begins thudding when he sees the silhouette of what Yee Lan is doing. First, the skirt. Then the unbuttoning of her blouse. Her bra, sliding off. Her panties being dropped. Teck Hin starts to tremble. "What are you doing?"

"Wasn't this what you wanted?" she asks.

"I ..."

"I saw your sketches of those nudes in your sketch pad. Isn't that what every artist wants? To draw naked women?"

A laugh, derisive and at the same time wondering, escapes him. Her innocence. Her attempt to please him. He puts a trembling hand against his neck. "Are you sure?" he says.

In answer, she comes out from behind the screen and takes his breath away.

* * *

He did draw Yee Lan nude. He drew her nude in many different poses, front and back, lying on a couch, playing with Dunia, looking coquettish, barely draped in linen. He drew her along a linear conception of art movements, from the Renaissance to the Impressionist to the Cubist and the Modern and then Postmodern. He drew her as solely lines and then in fragmented anatomy. He drew her with his moods and temperament, sometimes playful, sometimes romantic, sometimes in tarnished anger. He drew her until he began to understand himself, and in understanding himself, he began to understand Yee Lan's body, her physicality, as only he could. He saw what she did not see in herself. He saw, and the act of seeing and capturing an essence of Yee Lan in different mediums began to transform him; he felt himself tunnelling back in time towards a state of un-being, before rebirth. The more he knew, the more he had yet to know.

The painting he submitted to the Young Artist competition was a nude of Yee Lan. A full frontal nude of a young woman with an unmarked oval for a face – she is every orientalised woman that has ever been desired, every non-Western nude that has ever been painted, and she is faceless, subject to many interpretations: conceived and yet she does not exist, unknowable and unrecognisable.

Yee Lan viewed the portrait of herself hung up at the gallery for the art academy competition with a moue that turned into lips pressed together thinly and then slowly dissembled, the more she viewed herself. As she shifted the angle with which she viewed, at a certain point of perspective, she too began to understand.

And Aunty Boon Leng never found out.

About the Author

Elaine Chiew is a London-based writer and the editor/compiler of *Cooked Up: Food Fiction From Around The World* (New Internationalist, 2015). She won the Bridport Prize in 2008 and most recently the Elbow Room Prize (2015). She's been shortlisted in numerous competitions including Mslexia Short Story Competition, BBC Opening Lines, Fish International Short Stories Competition and nominated for the Pushcart Prize. Her stories can be found most recently in *Smokelong Quarterly* and *Unthology 7* (Unthank Books, 2015). She's currently pursuing an M.F.A. in Asian Art History in Singapore and has been travelling back and forth during 2016.

A BAD DECISION

DAMYANTI BISWAS

Nicole Lim had asked him for time. For a month, to be precise.

"We'll meet here, same time, same place, on February the 13th." She'd patted the café's smooth wooden table between them, discreetly, the way she did when trying to wake up a passenger traveling first class. That way, if things became unpleasant, she could volunteer to swap shifts with a colleague and fly on Valentine's Day.

"In the meantime," she said, "no messages, no calls. No contact."

He'd turned away from her, to gaze outside at the crowded crossing of Beach Road and Seah Street, not spoken for a while, his dark hands steepled together. His close-cropped hair had grown into the beginnings of grey-streaked curls, he wore rimless glasses on his large nose, his black skin still taut on his face, but his chin slightly sagged with the weight of the years. At sixty, Jesse Mosley was exactly twenty years older than her.

"All right," he'd leaned over to kiss her mouth, "but I already know what your answer will be."

In the last month, she'd thought of that kiss often. So self-assured, forceful, such a statement of ownership. And yet, such soft lips. Nicole's mother, *my name is Joanne, but you can call me*

Madam Lim, would have had a fit if she'd seen them. *Have some shame, girl, some things must do after marriage, okay? You want to make yourself cheap, what for, ah? A black man, some more.*

Nicole had suggested this TCC café because it made her feel secure on her own turf, a place where she came to wait it out when her mother had a day of check-ups at Raffles Hospital. A suitably neutral and public territory, in case she decided to turn him down. Right now though, she wished she'd chosen some place more private. The other patrons at the café, the whispering mothers with napping children, the elderly tourists in their caps and sneakers lingering over a late lunch, seemed too intrusive. What if she said yes? If she did, and he kissed her … She blushed, looked around, and let her long straight hair curtain her face. Oh, please. She sat up straighter and checked her pearl-strap watch.

In exactly two hours and twenty-five minutes, she had to give him an answer. She had taken a month to "think" about it. She would have jumped at his proposal if he'd asked her fifteen years ago, when she had never dreamed it possible. But now that he *had* asked her, divorced, eager, contrite at having wasted all the years they could have had together, she wanted to take it slowly.

A slim girl walked past the glass wall of the café, clad in a pencil skirt, ruffled top, a heavy designer bag slow-swinging on her arm. Staying thin cost Nicole more effort these days. A few years from now, they wouldn't renew her contract, no matter how good she looked. But she wouldn't get married simply because she was pushing forty and battling cellulite at the back of her still-firm thighs, though some women considered those excellent reasons. She pulled a small Moleskine notebook out of her handbag, turned a few pages, and using her fountain pen, drew a wavering black line down the centre of the page. "Pros", she wrote on the left, and on the right, "Cons".

She had to do this. Now. She stared at the words and resisted the urge to toss the notebook across the café. She needed words to fill both columns, but her mind had gone blank. The right answer might suggest itself when she set eyes on him again, much like a bout of sudden turbulence that hit the plane as she served lunch, nearly taking her off her feet. She had to use all her tricks not to keel over, or lose her smile.

She needed to stay rooted. She pressed the notebook flat on the table and wrote under Pros: *He's loaded. Can afford homes in three different continents.* Cons: *None. Really? Doesn't money come with its own set of problems?*

His money had brought them together the first time so many years ago at that conference, where she was a temp fresh out of school working with event planners, and he the chief speaker. In the early nineties, when smartphones seemed as much a possibility as colonising another planet, his limited edition phone had made an impression. Red and black phone in the shape of a Ferrari, it all but disappeared in his large dark hand as he spoke into it.

Nicole found it on the second day of the conference at his table while setting things right for the morrow. It was cold in her hand when she picked it up, small yet heavy like old Ming pottery. Its black buttons sat like shiny scarabs waiting for a touch to come awake and walk all over its glowing red body. She sat down with the phone in her hand, on his empty, still-warm chair. She put it to her ear and listened. She wished she could hear all it had to say, the conversations when his mouth near-kissed it at times.

All African-Americans (she had called him negro in her head, twenty years ago) had fat lips but his were shapely, the centre of his upper lip a perfect V, the lower a soft rounded pad she had imagined running her finger over.

She stood up when she heard a noise outside, her legs quaking. It wouldn't do to have someone come in and find her on his chair. She was about to put the phone back on the table when the door opened and he stepped in, spotted her standing in front of his chair, the little device still in her hand. He smiled, blinding-white teeth and twinkling eyes that said, *caught you*. She looked down and saw his red T-shirt falling over the slight bulge of his stomach, covering his almost-black jeans.

He had changed out of his beige suit, and she wasn't sure he knew how well his clothes matched his phone. On any other man, younger, smaller, less fleshed out, eyes less sharp, the whole effect would have been cheesy. Or maybe she was naïve then, and the raw pull of him was more to do with her inexperience.

Without a word, she'd handed him his phone, barely acknowledging his murmured thanks and his fingers that enveloped hers when the phone changed hands. The door rolled shut behind him and she stood breathing the silence, the vacuum created by his absence.

She raised her fingers to her cheek, transmitting his touch, the heat of it. Going back to his chair, she sank down and put her head on the table, recollecting the weight of the phone, as if in holding that phone she had held that body clad in red and black. She tried to lift her head, move it up little by little. She planned her actions: she would run her hands over her hair to make sure it was smooth, pick up sheaves of paper at the corner of the table and distribute them one by one on the chairs in front of her, all fifty-six of them. She'd straighten all the chairs, make sure the markers were in place, wipe the whiteboard clean. The slow-moving, white-haired cleaning lady had mopped the floors and left, promising to return after her tea to do anything else Nicole needed.

Instead of reaching for the papers though, she walked to the door. Or something walked her to it, because that was never her intention. She stepped outside to look down the deserted corridor. Only it wasn't empty. He stood by the side of the door, arms crossed, one knee bent, foot stuck to the wall behind him, in the stance of a much younger man. Waiting. She looked around but there was no one else about. He had waited for her, stood looking at her even as all the blood in her body rushed to her face, threatening to spill out of her pores. Her nerves refused to tell her abandoned limbs to move, and she stayed at the door, till he stepped towards her and they were both inside the conference hall, the door shutting behind them with a click.

They touched, whether it was he who first let his arm fall towards her or she who touched him with her eyes and drew him into that elastic invisible circle, where any movement was slow, awkward, the only moves that made sense were the ones they made towards each other. Through this haze, she paused once at the thought of the cleaner aunty coming back, but didn't move to stop him as he pushed her on top of a large table in the corner, his hands warm under her bare hips.

Afterwards, he helped her straighten her clothes and finish her work. Though they left the building separately, they spent the evening together, and the night, and nights after that till the conference ended. She stepped back once in a while, to consider exactly what she was doing with a married man, but being wanted by Jesse was like a drug in her blood. She became immune to all suggestions other than his.

His lecturing contract of two months came to an end, and he headed back to his family home in Washington. For the rest of the year, he called her during her night-time while he drove to work. She looked out of her window and tried to picture the sunlight through his windscreen, thrilled that she could have both daylight and darkness. His disembodied voice in her ears brought him close, taking her into his world, his frustration with colleagues, the traffic jam, but also his wonder at the wide fields of green or snow he drove past. Lying in bed she listened to him whisper what they could be doing right then if she were with him, making her blush under her sheets, glad it was dark, and that her mother lay fast asleep in the next room.

In the intervening years they met each time he taught at one of the various Singaporean colleges. He pushed her into applying for a spot in the elite crew of Singapore Airlines, and when she got in, she sent him her picture in her new uniform. Mother wasn't pleased. *Ah, just a waitress in the sky lah, Mei Mei, why you want to do this? You study so much for what?*

Later that year, when Nicole worked the Washington flight, he met her at the airport, and whisked her off to a hotel suite he'd booked, his smile strained, his thumb descending often on her knees in long strokes during the drive.

In the room, he coaxed her to bed without letting her take off the thigh-slitted uniform entirely, peeling it back for access instead.

"I've wanted to do this for so long," he gasped later, his hands on both sides of her as he moved.

"To an air hostess," she froze, "or me?"

"Both." He'd taken her mouth in a bruising kiss.

They met whenever they could over the next few years, and by the time she hit her late twenties, she pitied his wife, a pale figure she had created out of the words he let drop now and then. She also saw the way he looked at other women, slow-gazing at them the same way he ogled her when she wore a short dress. She never knew for sure, but Jesse didn't look content with cheating on his wife with one woman. He didn't seem to mind others. She didn't dare ask. She hated herself for going to him each time he crooked a finger, for waiting for his calls, falling for his surprises, aching to know what he was up to when she wasn't with him, for wanting him far more than he wanted her. For being young, for caring too much.

When a pilot asked her out, she said yes, and dropped Jesse. Others followed. A Singaporean air hostess never lacks for company and besides, Jesse had taught her well. She compared each man with Jesse, found them wanting, but took them on nevertheless. It was a physical thing between her and Jesse, it would wear out. One day, she'd see him, and he'd be an old man, and she'd wonder why she'd obsessed over him in the first place. She would laugh with him, at him, at his old-man, shrivelled smell.

When he called last year, Nicole was at a loose end, having separated from the Australian pilot she'd been dating for four years, and grown tired of. She couldn't stand pushovers after a while.

"Hey. What were you doing?" As if they'd spoken every day in the intervening years, or at least every week.

She had felt that familiar quickening of her heart, the dry mouth, that clench at the pit of her stomach. This part of her she couldn't control, the one that went to him, bushy tail wagging, ready for a pat. So much for laughing: his voice alone had undone her.

"Not much." She copied his bland tone. "You?" She was older now, did not, would not need him as bad.

"I land in four hours. Pick me up?"

Just like that. He hadn't asked her if she was with anyone else, assumed she'd drop everything the minute he called. He'd been right. At his hotel room, it hadn't been frantic as before, but what they lacked in speed, they made up for in skill. She tried to get away afterwards, but found herself listening as he spoke, their bare legs twined. He wanted to stay in Singapore for a while, he said. His wife had divorced him. He was considering retirement. He wanted to travel the world; with her, Nicole.

When she moved in with him to a rented apartment, her mother, predictably, had a meltdown.

How dare you live with a man in sin? What will I say to everyone at the reunion dinner?

Nicole had asked her mother to pipe down, not saying it in so many words, but meaning it: the Lim household now ran on Nicole's salary, not on her dead father's pension. Nicole paid for Madam Lim's treatments, for the occasional trip to Malacca and Penang to meet her sisters – Nicole's aunts who taunted her each Chinese New Year, *when are you going to start giving out* ang pow *instead of taking it?*

Nicole hadn't paid them heed in the last year of *living in sin* with Jesse. He travelled to Washington just once in that time, to celebrate the graduation of the youngest of his four children, the one who was born the year she met him. He took care of her cat each time she travelled, made her dinner way past midnight when she returned from a flight, brought her breakfast in bed on her days off.

And yet, when he asked her to marry him, she said, *I need time to think*, and moved back with her mother. *See, I told you it is no good*, her mother crowed and made chicken rice and pork rib-watercress soup for dinner, Nicole's favourites.

Fat good a month of her mother's food and her old bed had done her. Here she sat with her Moleskine notebook and coffee grown cold, staring out of the window and wondering what to do about it all.

She had one and a half hours to figure it all out. So the pen went back on the page, and under Pros she wrote: *Looks – okay for a sixty-year-old, slimmer than before. The glasses help. Now that he's older, he won't have a roving eye. Pretty sure that's why his wife divorced him.*

Under Cons: *Looks – People will say I married an older man for his money. I could find someone younger. He's not white. What will Mother say? Who'll take care of me in my old age?*

She crossed out that last line, blackening it out.

Her iPhone beeped. She took it out, checked her mail. On Facebook, she saw the album Jackie, a school friend, had uploaded: two little brats, identical twins in matching bibs. She flipped her Moleskine open again and under Pros she wrote: *Children – He adores children. Old age, low sperm counts not a problem these days.*

Cons: *He has four. Eldest is seven years younger than me.*

Won't be fun being stepmom. Our children might look funny, half-Singaporean, half-black.

Under Pros she scribbled: *Imagine how much those half-black kids would annoy Madam Lim. Would they have straight hair or curls? Haha. Take that, Mother.*

Nicole shut her notebook at this point, ordered another coffee. Think. Don't let emotions get the better of you.

Out on Beach Road, rush-hour traffic built up, and people walked by in a steady stream, couples, groups of college kids in colourful T-shirts, men and women on their own. Thoughts swarmed her like scarabs, but nothing of the sort seemed to bother the office-goers on their way home.

Under the column for Pros, she wrote: *Someone would wait for me, and it won't be Madam Lim!*

Cons: *What if he leaves me too, for someone else? Someone younger. Men don't age, they get better, bloody wiser. Hah. And I may settle for cooking him meals instead of launching a new career on land when I retire. Become his slave, do all the breakfasts-in-bed for him. Forgive him for cheating.*

Nicole worked her pen on that last bit till it punctured through the page. She pictured herself in Jesse's apartment off Orchard Road, waiting for him, or him waiting for her to return from a flight. After a month of not seeing him, no calls or messages, the idea of such a vigil had its appeal. She wrung her hands, then stopped, remembering her French-manicured nails. What if they just continued the way they were, *living in sin*, but no marriage?

Pros: *Mother can swan around at my wedding, and Madam Lim herself to her heart's content. Stupid goat aunties will shut up about the* ang pow.

Cons: *They'll say he's not the right match. Pah! Who cares what those old biddies think? But they could be right ...*

She looked up, and there stood the man she'd been agonising over, in a red polo-necked t-shirt draped over his broad shoulders, his perfect teeth, some of them false, beaming at her through the glass. He was early. She ground her lips into a smile. Had he remembered and worn that T-shirt on purpose? Had he thought about their first time way back then? To show her he hadn't changed?

He still thought he was young enough for other women. Earlier, Nicole couldn't protest, but as a wife, it wouldn't be the same. Their conversations flashed past her, their afternoons together in bed, the time he had turned up at the airport with a bouquet of lilies to surprise her and all the other hostesses had tittered and smiled. Another when they got wet in the rain, and he'd towelled her hair dry, made her coffee and then lunch, how once she'd cried on his shoulders when she broke up with one of her boyfriends ... Strange, how her mind zipped through a hundred images in less than a moment, in the space he smiled at her and pushed the door open. If she said yes, she would replace the pale figure, his long-suffering wife who had divorced him five years ago. Why had he waited four years to call?

Maybe she could put him off for today. She was getting carried away, making a bad decision. The scarabs inside her head moved in for the kill.

She didn't rise, but she knew her eyes shone, that she sat straight up, legs a little un-crossed under her mini-skirt, face raised for his kiss of greeting on her cheek. Her smile didn't waver; she knew her answer.

About the Author

Damyanti's short fiction has been commended at the Bath Flash Fiction Award. Her novel-in-progress was long-listed for the Mslexia Novel Competition and Bath Novel Award. Her stories appear at *Bluestem*, *Griffith Review*, *Lunch Ticket*, among others, and anthologies in the USA, Malaysia and Singapore.

A LONG BICYCLE RIDE
INTO THE SEA

JON GRESHAM

Immediately after completing my law degree, I met a girl who changed my life. She laughed at my jokes, and as a consequence I was deluded enough to believe that she understood the incomprehensible depths of my soul.

I have false and abiding memories of lilac-flavoured kisses, forget-me-not smiles, holding hands and velvet speeches. The truth is, none of that happened. Instead, I sought her and, following the four greatest mistakes of my life and a series of desperate interactions climaxing in an extravagant lunge for her affections, I cycled beyond the coast and into the sea for her.

Whatever fleeting intimacy we shared meant much, much more to me than to her. Our relationship was like the wind. Not an epic, swirling east wind that arrives from across the sea and bears down on the city, ushering in thunder and rain, but the kind of wind that tends to escape an individual at the most awkward of moments. At first there is laughter, but then the smell reaches the nose and there is only an enduring discomfort.

It all began when I went to work at a small law firm in Tanjong Pagar for six weeks before heading to a prestigious law firm in

London. I spent my time thinking of England and dreaming of her while staring out the rear window of the shophouse where the firm carried out its conveyancing practice. Back then, I was in between days; all I had to do was last six weeks until I took a plane to England and an internship at the venerable London law firm of Messrs Johnson, Slasher and Eaglebottom, specialists in maritime insolvency. I was on the cusp of a career and I couldn't wait to get out and start life in earnest.

However, before I could get to England, I had to hang around for a while, coasting along at a dead-end job, because I didn't have enough money to travel (having spent lavishly on my wardrobe) and detested moping about at home. So it was at this grey place that I met her and worked for Mr Tan, Managing Partner of Tan & Tan, conveyancing and probate at half the price.

I first entered Mr Tan's offices (looking damn spiffy, if I don't say so myself) wearing my Prada suit; a wide-lapelled, double button-down collared shirt from Raoul with onyx cufflinks; a shiny pair of Lloyds; and my hair zapped upwards with a splodge of styling gel. And then I saw her by the photocopier and she walked towards me. She wore a black pencil skirt, a white silk blouse with her hair tied back in a neat ponytail, and black Louboutin heels. As she shook my hand and introduced herself, I felt like I'd seen her somewhere before. I saw on her wrist a silver bracelet from which jangled several small charms: a starfish, a heart, an English thatched cottage, a Scottish terrier, and a lobster.

That first time she smiled at me ... well ... she saw straight through all my pretensions and yet she seemed to quite like me. That is what made her so attractive. She seemed to see people as they were. I really thought she "got" me. She floated above the surface of things, sprinkling about a quiet joy. Later, when we got to know each other, we laughed a great deal; I felt like Benny Hill flirting with Emily Dickinson.

On my first day, I sat at my desk staring out the window, daydreaming about her, ignoring piles of documents while speculating on her origins and the connection between dogs and crustaceans. My window faced onto the back alley and the rear of a row of shophouses containing a series of exotic karaoke lounges, beer bars and Halal eating houses. I thought of her while staring vacantly at the backside of air-conditioning units, concrete spiral staircases, and the piss and vomit stains from the night before. As the afternoon grew late, I gazed upwards beyond the birdcages and bougainvilleas on the balcony and caught glimpses of karaoke girls getting ready in upstairs rooms.

I liked and lusted after her a lot. I imagined her at home in a decent HDB flat in Clementi, living an ordinary life with her evangelical Christian parents and her chubby, vision-impaired little brother. In the beginning, I circled around her without speaking – which was pretty hard in that small, dull office. Eventually, after several days, I contrived to bump into her by the water cooler. Alas, my withering wit went fishing. I said something like, "How … er … er … How is the water today?" She looked at me, smiled, and walked away without saying anything. Later, in the bathroom mirror, I noticed a little speck of chilli stuck between my teeth.

She became tangled up inside my head like a thousand strands of vermicelli. My story is an effort to untangle that mess; it's not really about her as a person, more about the image, the aftertaste, the lingering fragrance, my "what ifs" of her. There is something so lost and pathetic about these memories and desires;

these fragments of my sad, younger life yearnings, scribbled dreams, strains of vain overconfidence and failed attempts to reach beyond mediocrity. But I cannot help wading through them time and again, seeking to discover some meaning from the events of that summer.

Mr Tan caught me staring at her and said, "That girl is a portal to hell."

Mr Tan was squat, tubby and bald. He warned me against having anything to do with her. He sat behind a huge desk in his office surrounded by plastic orchids and cardboard boxes full of red-ribboned files beneath a large ebony-framed painting of a beautiful woman with an enormous bouffant. He told me that the lady in the picture was his late wife, a famous Singaporean singer who'd drowned in a boating accident. He blinked more than most people and spoke like a Hokkien SpongeBob SquarePants. He laughed at me. "Don't look at me as your boss but as your friend. I'm telling you to stay away from her because I don't want you to get hurt." He smiled and I saw tobacco-stained teeth and, at the back of his mouth, fillings like black flies sleeping on pieces of popcorn. A wave of halitosis hit me. Even when his mouth was closed there was an air of molasses and Dettol about him.

Mr Tan had been a conveyancing lawyer since before Independence. He was also an expert on karaoke lounges of dubious repute and the best places to get cheese and mushroom *roti prata* at five in the morning. By way of orientation on one of my first days at the office, Mr Tan took me to the *kopitiam* around the corner and gave me a rundown on the firm. At the end of the briefing he said, "I know you're only here for six weeks but make the most of it because when you fail at your big firm in London you can always come back here. Hahaha." Then he started to talk about karaoke: "There is nothing like a dark shophouse full of ballads, lovely ladies, lots of beer and pissing in the back alley with your friends." He told me about recent advances in lights, consoles and microphones. He lamented that it was only a matter of time before 3-D holograms hit the lounges: "You look at technology now and compare it to when we were kids. You look back at all the changes in your life and how, materially speaking, we've progressed. But the fun in simple things never changes. Thank God people always need to transfer property and sing songs with real ladies. Hahaha."

I spent my days completing conveyancing checklists, reconciling trust accounts and preparing property tax notifications. My life was full of so many flat shades of grey. Everything reeked of a quiet desperation and I determined not to let any of it rub off. I was dying of boredom and my only relief was staring out the back window, dreaming about her and waiting for the late afternoon when I could see the karaoke girls preening themselves before work. As the day became evening, I watched from across the alleyway as the girls got ready in their underwear, puffing up their hair and applying eyelashes before ironing short sequined dresses.

After the water cooler incident, I spent a lot of time thinking of questions to seduce her: "How do you get double-sided duplicates on this photocopier? Do you like a cinnamon stick in your latte? Have you considered Belle and Sebastian?" But I didn't need to use any of these strategies as she walked over to my desk one day and asked if I would like to have lunch with her at Lau Pa Sat.

So we lunched at Lau Pa Sat and talked through the surface

of our lives. I told her my glorious pretensions and she smiled back with a charming reticence. I asked her what she was doing working for Mr Tan? Surely she could find something better? She said it's just a job and she was biding her time while readying her heart and soul for the Universe. I told her I could relate to that. We talked about the dreariness of everyday life, how most things were old cabbage and wet socks. I told her I was getting out, moving to London where I could lose myself. I lectured her on the courage to move away from one's comfort zone. She smiled at me and suggested Lombok rather than London.

After that first lunch, I really felt comfortable with her. It seemed we shared something special. We had lunch almost every other day, eating a variety of hawker fare: chicken and beef satay, mutton soup, grilled swordfish, oyster omelettes, Taiwanese noodles, and tapioca and sweetcorn desserts.

We held a number of extended conversations. Over durian ice cream we argued about who would win an all-in tag team wrestling match between Wayne Rooney and Fernando Torres, Amitabh Bachchan and Maggie Q, Kong Hee and Lawrence Khong. Over cheese and onion *roti prata* we pondered why cats are arrogant and how dogs learn empathy.

She talked about the ways in which everything is connected to everything; that the lungs are an extension of the air in which you live and move around. She said no person is an island. So I asked, "What are we then? Continents? Planets? Solar systems?" Later, she told me we were car parks, where the self is just a little bit of grey concrete marked out by painted white lines and we define ourselves by who we let drive in and how long they stay.

She talked about Ai Weiwei, Miroslav Tichý, Henry Darger

and Beatrix Potter and how wonderful it was to be lost in your own massive inner world. She said I reminded her of a cross between Justin Bieber and Taufik Batisah.

We both looked forward to our time together but she wouldn't let me see her after work or on the weekends. This didn't deter me because I felt our lunches were so wonderful and one day, someday, she would eventually relent and let me take her on a real date. Around the office we didn't speak very much at all. It was difficult with Mr Tan lurking about. It was such a quiet office except for the whirr of fans, the stuttering drone of the air-conditioning, the gurgle of the water cooler and the occasional client. She smiled at me every time she caught me looking at her.

The conversation at lunch would occasionally turn to our employer. I asked why he had so many bottles of alcohol-based hand sanitiser around the office and what was behind his obsession with karaoke? She smiled even more, as though she knew something I didn't.

At lunch one day I told her, "I still don't know why someone like you works for Mr Tan. You're like a character that's entered stage left into the wrong play. Instead of you leaving hurriedly or being kicked out, everyone – the other actors, the director, the playwright, and even the makeup artist – begs you to stay because you illuminate everything and get more laughs and inject more soul into their play than they can themselves." She told me to stop making her puke.

She leant forward towards me to grab a small plastic spoon from my side of the table. As she reached over I caught a fleeting glimpse of the curve of her breast and the warm brown of her left nipple beyond the folds of her cotton blouse and slightly too large, padded bra. At that precise moment, I committed the first greatest mistake of my life and fell completely in love with her.

I began to think seriously about taking her to London. In the afternoons after lunch, I watched the karaoke girls get ready as I let the humidity, boredom and heat wash over me. I imagined the inside of her dreams, vertiginous rainbow caverns with fruit bats bouncing about between glitter balls and stalactites dripping liquid silver chocolate onto Scottish terriers.

Sadly, she gave the impression that she would never leave that office. She seemed a constant fixture, loving the stability of hating a boring, mundane job while embracing the anarchy and restlessness of her inner life. I thought she lacked the courage to move beyond her comfort zone. I thought she'd prefer to be free in the mind rather than, like the rest of us, actually doing something, trying and failing ... and, eventually, finding out we have to let go of our dreams. I wondered what she'd say if I asked her to come to England with me.

A week before I was due to leave for London, we were at lunch at Lau Pa Sat and she told me she was handing in her resignation. I looked up from my deep-fried pork. I was stunned. She touched her hair, she smiled, and the skin wrinkled ever-so-slightly across the bridge of her nose.

I said, "Wow! That's great. What for? What are you doing ... Er ... Why?"

She laughed. "Well. I need to get away."

"Great," I said. "Come with me to London."

"No," she said. "No. I can't." She smiled ever-so-slowly at me. Then I committed the second greatest mistake of my life:

I tried to kiss her.

I keep playing the memory of this episode in a loop through my mind, over and over again. I'm stuck in this everlasting prelude to a kiss. Working up the courage but doing nothing, until I decide to do it and I lean forward, eyes closed, tentatively aiming my lips at her lips. Waiting, feeling for a signal, for permission that I can actually kiss her ... and I don't get that signal, so I pull back. At that particular microsecond she leans forward, but it's too late to go back in, and as I pull out she picks up on my hesitation, so she pulls out too ... and the moment is lost.

Then, to try and capture something amongst the debris of this missed kiss, I made the third greatest mistake of my life:

I told her I loved her. She looked at me and didn't say anything – playing, for quite a time, with the marrow in her mutton soup.

"I love you." There, I said it again.

She replied, "My God! Are you from the Planet Zog? Come on. No you don't. You see me like those Asian airline stewardesses in adverts, a Western male fantasy of Asian women ... an always-smiling, demure, malleable, acquiescent slave. You don't see the real me. Do you realise how much you're insulting me?"

I objected strongly and mumbled something about being Eurasian, about not being a representative Western male, and exclaimed that we needed each other to defeat the drabness lapping at our lives.

She said, "You need to be shocked into seeing things as they are. I think what you need is a long bicycle ride into the sea."

I looked at her, puzzled. What was she on about?

"It's like an extreme cold shower. But you do it fully clothed. The resistance. The pressure. Your trousers balloon, fill up with air, and you try to trundle onwards. But your wheels sink in the sand, the water rises around your waist and your balls shrink to the size of peas. And then you end up falling sideways, plopping into the sea."

I sat there thinking, what kind of a challenge is this? What good was it supposed to do anyone? Why should I cycle into the sea for her? It wasn't a question about whether she was worth it. It was more about whether I could handle the absurd nature of the act. It was all so useless and silly. There was no connection between love and cycling into the sea. But she said it had the most intense meaning just because it was so totally irrational.

She got up, looked at me sitting there, and told me if I really loved anyone enough, then I'd get a taxi to the East Coast and take a long bicycle ride into the sea for them. She left and headed back to the office.

As I watched her leave, I realised if she was going to be mine then I'd have to take up this challenge. There was no going back. I had committed to someone and was compelled to demonstrate the depth of my feelings and the courage and coolness of my eccentricities.

So, a week later, on my last day of work, I took the afternoon off and I was at the East Coast with a bicycle. I wore Speedos underneath my trousers.

She hadn't come in to work that whole week and she wasn't responding to my emails, tweets or wall posts. I left a message inviting her along and providing precise location and time details. When I arrived, she was nowhere to be seen. I waited there, silently staring out to sea for a long, long time until eventually, in the soft early evening light, I decided she was a no-show but I'd have to do it anyway. Never mind, I thought, it's better if we speak after I return. Even though I would be wet ... I would be victorious.

I mounted the bicycle and rode towards the sea and onto the sand, cycling past chilli crab restaurants, dog-walking couples and rollerblading singles. I rolled over firm, damp sand and I kept telling myself, if you do this you will truly see who you are. I kept heading towards the line of the horizon. The water started to soak the bottom of my trousers, my shoes squelched as I pedalled, and my socks were soggy.

As I progressed into the water I told myself, although strange, this wasn't as bad as it sounds; a bit like pushing a cotton bud in too far and thinking you've touched brain. The water was murky like miso soup. I saw bits floating about. I had this incredible sense of going with the flow. Then I was struck by a crisis of confidence as the resistance grew and thoughts of large dry-cleaning bills loomed before me. I was slowing and hesitant. I had to keep bolstering myself with clichés: Don't worry, keep going. It's worth it. It will get the girl. I'm okay. It's okay. If you get knocked down, you'll get up again. If it doesn't kill you, it will make you stronger. My legs ached and I felt a sharp pain across my chest. The wheels of the bicycle were almost at a stop and the water was above my waist.

Then I turned to look back towards the shore and I thought I saw her standing there, quietly watching me bicycle into the sea. I raised my arm to wave but I fell sideways, my head went under and I found myself thrashing about beneath the surface. I was totally immersed and my legs and trousers were tangled up in the pedals and chain. She was there in my mind with the salt water flooding up my nose, and I became the small silver lobster on her charm bracelet all boiled up in her.

I resurfaced and emerged from the water humiliated and invigorated. I left the bicycle behind somewhere at the bottom of the sea about twenty metres off the East Coast. It's probably still there. I felt baptised, changed ... alive. A seagull flew overhead and the person I thought was her was no longer there. I took a taxi to Mr Tan's office. I was wet but happy and wanted to share my achievement with her. I wanted her to know that I'd broken through and performed a stupid feat to let the universe know that choices exist, nothing is normal and that I loved her.

It was late evening and the light had already faded when I arrived at Mr Tan's office. The office was closed. Everyone had gone home. No worries, I thought, I'll catch her tomorrow just before I leave for London. It was then I committed the fourth greatest mistake of my life. Instead of following the sensible path and going home to change out of my wet clothes, I decided to visit the karaoke lounge behind Mr Tan's office. I told myself I might never get the chance to visit a Tanjong Pagar karaoke lounge ever again and I needed a stiff drink to warm up.

I walked past smiling ladies in fraying cheongsams standing in the five-foot way smoking cigarettes and into the Silver Charms karaoke lounge. I entered a large room with plush red carpet on the walls, dark vinyl booths, and a raised podium in the far corner where some girl was singing "无条件为你" ("Unconditionally for You") robustly and off-key. The lounge was loud, musty and hazy. It was busy with lots of blokes. Smoke lingered from cigarettes and Filipino cigars. It was hard to see as the only light came from lasers flashing coloured lines across the room and the glow of TV screens showing balls bouncing across the tops of lyrics as couples walked through tulip gardens. I wondered about trying to find a drink. Then I saw Mr Tan seated on the edge of a vinyl seat in the corner of the room. He was wearing a beige safari suit with a burgundy silk handkerchief flopping raffishly from his left breast pocket. On his feet was a pair of bright new Hush Puppies. He was surrounded by a raucous bunch of rotund middle-aged men, all with dyed hair and a drink in hand. You could tell they'd been drinking a lot by the amount of spit coming out of their mouths when they laughed.

Mr Tan, at the front of the booth, was more subdued. He had a strange angelic leer on his face. He was staring intently at the lady singing on the podium in the corner of the room. He watched her in a way I'd never seen anybody watch before or since.

I focused my gaze and I saw an elegant lady in full flight, singing at the top of her voice from the bottom of her chest. The strength of her voice contrasted with her poise and petite figure. I remember thinking, who would have thought someone looking like that could sing so loudly and yet so off-pitch? Mr Tan appeared transfixed, as though hypnotised. She wore glitter eye shadow and ruby red lipstick. Her hair cascaded down upon her bare neck. She wore an off-the-shoulder silver sequined dress, a silver necklace, and a silver charm bracelet on her wrist from which jangled the tiniest cottage, Scottish terrier and lobster. I was stunned. She touched her hair, she smiled, and the skin wrinkled ever-so-slightly across the bridge of her nose.

She stepped off the small stage at the corner of the room and walked towards Mr Tan. She leant towards him and, with one hand clasping the thick microphone, she held the other to his face. With her fingertips, she touched him lightly on the cheek.

I watched as Mr Tan held his whisky glass in one hand and raised the other towards her. He brought the back of his fingers to her face where he let them linger, and he stroked with the slightest, softest touch. Not once did they stop looking at each other.

That was all some time ago, and now I am losing myself in damp, cold London. I spend my long afternoons at work trying not to think about those days. However, recently I googled "a long bicycle ride into the sea", hoping to find links to freedom and Tanjong Pagar karaoke girls getting ready for an evening's entertainment. Instead, my browser crashed as I ended up unable to click past invitations to video chats with Stacey from Bermondsey and Crystal from Hainan.

It is then that I remember clearly the way they looked at each other, and I still cannot tell whether they were lovers, father and daughter, or both.

About the Author

Jon Gresham is a writer living in Singapore. His stories have been published in various literary journals and anthologies, including *Quarterly Literary Review Singapore*, *Eastern Heathens*, *Coast* and *From the Belly of the Cat*. He writes stories, takes photographs and blogs at www.igloomelts.com. His debut collection of short stories, *We Rose Up Slowly*, was published in 2015.

"A Long Bicycle Ride into the Sea" was previously published in *We Rose Up Slowly* by Jon Gresham (Singapore: Math Paper Press, 2015) and *Coast: Fifty-Three Works Titled Coast, A Mono-Titular Anthology of Singapore Writing* edited by Daren Shiau and Lee Wei Fen (Singapore: Math Paper Press, 2011).

Ex

VERENA TAY

Today's an on-track day, Wong thinks as he receives the $50 note that his passenger just used to pay his fare. He returns the change and the man exits the cab to stride into Plaza Singapura. Driving all morning, Wong has made enough to cover his taxi rental and fuel costs for the day. The afternoon earnings will be pure profit, useful for paying the baby's doctor fees and the new laptop for his older son. *One more job. Then lunch. Busy dads must also eat,* mulls Wong, glancing at the acrylic-framed photo of his family on the dashboard.

He loves the picture taken about a month ago, a proper studio shot to celebrate the second anniversary of his marriage to Ying. In the photo, Ying, plump and beautiful, sits next to him. Her arms are filled with their chubby infant son, Bin. Behind stands Wei, gangly with teenage attitude, his son from his first marriage. What a beautiful image. A real, complete family that he has battled the odds to create. His family for whom he is determined to walk the straight and narrow and work hard to protect.

Wong quickly checks his mobile phone for an update about Bin's appointment with the paediatrician. He is so engrossed with his wife's message that he hardly pays attention to the couple hopping into the backseat of his taxi until the woman says,

"Geylang Lorong 8." His heart sinks momentarily at the need to drive through his former haunts of the bad old days. Then something about the woman's voice catches his attention. The slurred quality is familiar in its high-pitched nasality. Before he pulls away from the taxi stand, Wong peers at his new passengers through the rear-view mirror. He does not know the man, but he definitely knows the woman.

It is Lee Lee. Same tousled, centre-parted, shoulder-length hair. Same high forehead. Same button nose. Same protruding eyes. Same figure-hugging, mini-skirted dress sense. Same snuggling too close to her man with her hand stroking his thigh ever so near his crotch. But the ten years since Wong last saw her have not been kind. Now her hair is lank and obviously dyed, her forehead wrinkled, her body too saggy to look decent in such a dress. Her skin is bad, her cheeks are haggard, her eyes are demon wild and her actions are fidgety: sure signs that she is back to her old ways, despite repeated stints in prison and drug rehab.

The sight of his ex-wife shakes Wong deeply. *Wah lan eh! What are the chances of Lee Lee getting into my cab? How can this happen? My day now kaput! My future all kaput!* Apart from whatever distaste he has for her, he is nervous and the anxiety is genuine. He used to live in hell like her. In fact, she was one of the reasons why he stayed there for years. Eventually he clawed his way out and found his reasons to stay out. But sadly, once a resident of hell, one can never truly escape, for hell will always be only a step away. One sure way back is to mix with former company. In his head, Wong hears what various counsellors have drilled into him: "Avoid old friends. If you meet them, be careful. Be strong. Don't let them drag you back." *Hah! Be strong? Right now, better avoid.* Abruptly, he stops looking at the mirror and drives away from Plaza Singapura, hoping to remain silently anonymous for the duration of the journey.

The sudden movement of his eyes and the lurch of the taxi prove to be his undoing. The woman shifts her attention and looks at her taxi driver via the rear-view mirror. Recognition slowly dawns on her. Thrilled, she unwraps herself from her companion, leans forward, and asks, "Ah Wong?"

Aiyah, why was I so nosy? Too late. Now, must be polite. Wong smiles tightly, answering, "Hello, Lee Lee."

"Wah, you look so different!"

"You've not changed much."

"Aiyah, old already," she titters, accepting his response as a compliment.

"How are you?"

"Okay, lah. Ah Heng, Ah Heng! This is Wong! I tell you about him many times. Wong, my fiancé, Heng!"

Through the rear-view mirror, Wong glimpses at Heng. The man is as surly as he is brawny. He acknowledges Wong with a curt nod and then frowns, obviously displeased with Lee Lee's eager chatter. Wong discreetly nods back. From past experiences with tough-guy gangster types like Heng, he guesses his ex-wife's fiancé must be a bouncer, pimp, pusher or a combination of the three. Since Heng is not a man to be trifled with, Wong is even more wary of keeping his distance.

Oblivious to her present surroundings and forgetful of the past, Lee Lee prattles on, seeking greater intimacy, "I hear you become clean. But I never believe until today. Look at you! Not like last time. Now so proper! You put on weight, wear business

EX

shirt, business pants, business shoes. Like towkay. Drive your own cab! You earn a lot?"

"Can do."

"Hey, you got card!"

Lee Lee spots his open box of name cards that he displays on the armrest between the driver's and front passenger's seats. For the first time in his five years of taxi driving, Wong regrets the use of this marketing tactic. *Alamak! What if she, or that man, calls me anytime, anywhere?* Then he tries to reassure himself. *Don't worry. Business is business. Nothing will happen.*

Lee helps herself to several cards. "I take, okay? Next time, I need taxi, Heng need taxi, we call you! See, Ah Heng, today we so lucky! Bump into Wong. Now we have private chauffeur. Heeheeheehee ..."

Heng grunts, impatient with her behaviour. Lee Lee ignores him as something else grabs her attention: the family photo on the dashboard. She squeals, "Wong, your new wife, is it? So pretty! Your baby, so cute!"

Then her high-pitched patter stops for a second. In contrast, her next question is quiet and sober. "Is that Wei?" she asks, pointing to their son's image in the picture.

"Yah."

"Can I see?"

Wong resists, old prejudices and memories returning. *No! You gave birth to him in prison and abandoned him! I had to fight the courts to get him! You've no right to see him or claim him.*

"Please?"

The softness of her plea makes him realise how irrational his thoughts are. *She is Wei's mother after all. She's not seen him in*

75

over ten years. Of course she's curious. Why am I worried? I've got full custody. If I say no, she can't touch him. Half-heartedly, Wong lifts the photo frame away from the anti-slip mat on the dashboard and hands the picture to Lee Lee.

She sits back to pore over the photograph. His eyes on the road, Wong cannot see Lee Lee's reaction. Instead, he hears her saying softly, "So big already. So handsome. So tall."

Her mutterings must have irritated Heng, for the gangster interrupts brusquely, "You see what?"

Through the rear-view mirror, Wong notices Lee Lee turning towards Heng and showing him the picture. She points and says, "My son."

Heng takes hold of the photo and peers at it. Then the gangster snorts so dismissively that Wong feels offended. *Why you think my son is nothing when you've never even met him in real life?* Then he realises that the sound is directed at Lee Lee, not him. The sound implied, "Your old life doesn't count anymore. I am all that matters now. Pay attention to me, or else ..." The sound is a sign that Lee Lee finally heeds as she becomes quiet.

At first, Wong is relieved that Lee Lee has stopped talking. Then the silence lengthens and he senses the unnaturalness of the hush. When he halts the taxi at a red traffic light, Wong checks the mirror to see what is going on in the backseat. He observes Lee Lee shrunken like a deflated balloon. Before Wong can react, Heng leans forward to return the picture, blocking the disturbing view of Lee Lee. Wong receives the photo awkwardly, replaces it on the dashboard and then glances again at the rear-view mirror. Seated back, Heng jerks his chin at Lee Lee, beckoning her. Immediately, she scuttles across the backseat and curls up by the gangster's side, assuming the position that she started the journey with. As a final touch, Heng places a possessive arm over his fiancée.

What he witnesses so bewilders Wong that he does not realise the light has turned green until the cars behind the taxi honk at him. Quickly, he drives forward with his mind whirling. *Wah piang eh! You want her, you keep her! It's not as if I like her anymore.* Yet he must admit his concern. *What happened to her? Why is she so quiet, so obedient? The old Lee Lee used to talk and talk and talk, do things her own way, argue with people all the time, all over the place! Who is this man? How did he turn her into a pet? Why does she let him control her?*

As he wonders whether he should do or say something, some perspective returns to him. At the next stoplight, Wong notices a bus ad promoting baby formula. Instead of the model infant, Wong sees Bin's roly-poly, smiling face within the poster. He turns his focus back inside his cab towards the precious picture of his family. Ying, Bin and Wei stare back at him. Once again, he is aware of where his priorities lie. *I cut ties with Lee Lee a long time ago. Her relationship with Heng is none of my business. If I get involved, I will destroy my new life and put my family in danger. How can I let my sons grow up without a father? Who will look after Ying if I am not around? No. Back off. Stay out.*

For the rest of the journey, silence continues to reign in the back seat. Wong no longer checks behind. Instead within his head, he continually repeats the mantra: *Be strong. Be strong. Be strong.* His concentration only breaks at Geylang Lorong 8 when Heng tells Wong to stop the taxi beside a cheap hotel.

Heng pays the fare and steps out of the cab without a further word. He holds the door open for Lee Lee. Dutifully, she scrambles towards the exit. Before she leaves, she turns and waves goodbye in a tiny, almost imperceptible gesture. Despite his better judgement, the little movement tugs Wong's heart. He cannot help saying to her, "Good to see you. You got my card. You need anything, call yah?" Lee Lee flashes him the biggest grin he has ever seen from her. And then she is gone.

Over the next few weeks, Wong lives in terror that he will hear from Lee Lee or Heng. Fortunately, the dreaded call never comes and the fear subsides. Weeks turn into months and the memory of meeting his ex-wife fades in Wong's head as the more pressing concerns of how to make a living and look after his family take precedence.

About a year later, Wong is ending the day shift. While handing his taxi over to the relief driver, Wong receives a call on his mobile phone.

"Good afternoon, is this Mr Wong Mun Kit?"

"Yes."

"Mr Wong, you are the father of Wong Wei Liang and your first wife was Ang Lee Lee?"

"Yes. Who are you?"

"I beg your pardon, Mr Wong. I am calling on behalf of the Public Trustee's Office. I regret to inform you that Ang Lee Lee has passed on …"

Even though Wong knows the dangers of the world that Lee Lee was living in, the suddenness of the news of her death shocks him and he barely registers that Wei will be inheriting what little property she has left behind. Later, when he is calmer, he checks through the old grapevine and learns that she and Heng were found dead in a Bedok flat several months previously, both overdosed on coke.

The news confuses him. *Wah piang eh! Thank God I'm still alive and out of that shit. Kan ni na! Why did she die? Why she never escape? Why didn't I help?* In his mind, Wong replays the scene of when he last saw her again and again. *Maybe I shouldn't have been so afraid for myself. Maybe I should've done something instead.* Then he recalls his final image of her. *Why did she smile like that? Did I make her day then? Aiyah! Now how to know ...*

There is only one thing to do now. Before making his way back to his twelfth-floor, three-room flat in Yishun, Wong drops by the neighbourhood provision shop to buy some joss sticks and paper money. At home, he prepares the small family brazier on the common corridor outside the flat with Ying standing in the front doorway and looking on curiously with Bin in her arms. Minutes later, Wei slouches down the corridor from the lift back from school, his backpack slung over one shoulder and his eyes and fingers glued to his smartphone. Wong calls out, "Wei!"

"Ah Pa. What's wrong?"

"Your mother died."

"But Ying is ..." Wei gestures towards his stepmother.

"Your birth mother."

"Oh."

The lack of interest on his son's face does not deter Wong. "Come, Wei," commands Wong, "pay your respects." He takes hold of Wei's phone and bag, putting them by the front door next to Ying. He picks up a box of matches he had earlier placed beside the brazier and gives the matches to Wei, indicating that his son should light the paper money placed within.

Reluctantly, Wei does as he is instructed and the offering

catches fire. Wong hands Wei more hell notes to burn. The smoke and ash rise. Wei coughs and Wong notices how much his son's forehead and nose resembles those of his mother. It seems like Lee Lee is standing next to him, not his son.

When all of the hell notes have been fed to the fire, Wong lights a joss stick each for himself and for Wei. Turning to face open air beyond the common corridor parapet, Wei, at Wong's command, stiffly bows three times towards the sky with his joss stick between his hands. The duty done, he places the joss stick into the holder next to the front door of the flat and looks expectantly at his father. Wong sighs and says, "Good boy. Now go inside and eat your dinner."

Wei greets his stepmother and enters his home, picking up his belongings in the process. Ying, still holding her child in her arms, follows Wei inside to set out the meal. Left alone, Wong bows, the smoke from his joss stick sending skyward his silent mantra of *Lee Lee, be at peace.*

About the Author

As a writer and editor, Verena Tay (www.verenatay.com) has published two short story collections – *Spaces: People/Places* (2016) and *Spectre: Stories from Dark to Light* (2012) – and four play collections, and edited various fiction anthologies, including the popular *Balik Kampung* series published by Math Paper Press. An Honorary Fellow at the International Writing Program, University of Iowa (Aug–Nov 2007), she holds Masters degrees in English Literature, Voice Studies and Creative Writing. She is currently pursuing her PhD in Creative Writing at Swansea University.

"Ex" was previously published in *Spaces: People/Places* by Verena Tay (Singapore: Math Paper Press, 2016) and, in a shortened format, in *Passages* (Singapore Writers Festival 2013).

TRUE NORTH

SHOLA OLOWU-ASANTE

Laser treatment promised results and the DeepLite 350 made bold claims, effective, even on black skin. But after six sessions in as many months – she would need ten in total – Buki had seen little change. The offending image still sat on her arm, like a guest that had overstayed their welcome. Still she made the MRT journey across town from Kallang to Orchard each month to sit in the faux leather recliner in Shu Mei's starkly lit treatment room in Far East Plaza. Somewhere along the line, they became friends, in the kind of random and spontaneous manner that had only ever happened to her in Singapore. So Buki didn't blame Shu Mei for the lack of progress.

Of the three dermatologists she had spoken to, only Shu Mei had been willing to work on skin as dark as hers. With her feathery eyebrows and pockmarked face, she was hardly a poster girl for her profession but she talked as much as a taxi uncle, which Buki found a comfort. Sure, Shu Mei was indiscreet and Buki had heard too many stories about other clients to think that her own confidence was being kept. All that mattered was Shu Mei was cheap and did not complain when Buki squirmed like a five-year-old, begging for a time-out.

"You want to take a break already?"

The machine, a touch screen monitor perched above a tower that looked like an upright air-conditioning unit, hummed and hissed. Buki took short shallow breaths. Some said it felt like a hot rubber band being snapped against the skin but for Buki it felt more like being stabbed with a needle. Hundreds of little pin pricks moving across her arm in rapid succession. She had tried visualisation techniques and chewing gum, but she had yet to sit through an entire session without whining for Shu Mei to stop.

"Keep going. I'll try and last another five minutes."

"See! You're getting used to it. Nothing like my new client last week. Thirty seconds and he was almost crying. Guess where he placed his tattoo?"

"His calf."

"Noooo," Shu Mei said, with a look that made her eyebrows shimmy.

"I don't know. His neck? His eyelids?"

Shu Mei pulled the laser away from Buki's arm and used it to gesture at her belt.

"No way!" Buki squealed. "Not on his ..."

"Noooo. Not on. Just above. It says 'U Lucky Bitch'! Haha! Can you imagine?"

"Oh my God ..."

"But there's more."

"It can't possibly get any worse."

"Yes," Shu Mei she said with glee. "There's an arrow! Pointing south!"

The two women doubled over with laughter that spun and ricocheted across the walls. *Poor sod*, Buki thought, before falling back into silence and a well of self-pity. It wasn't as if her own ink was any less ridiculous. Two naked lovers wrapped with vines and "BUKI & DAVID FOREVER" printed beneath.

The machine continued its snap-snapping above her skin. Buki gritted her teeth. Shu Mei bent towards her and Buki could see the follicles in her scalp, smell the lunch-hour durian on her breath. She was blathering on now. Something about ghosts and closets.

"I don't believe in ghosts," Buki said.

"You've just never met a real one before," Shu Mei said, leaning in closer still. "But this one rattles away inside my Ah Ma's wooden chest most nights. She died last year. I think maybe she is trying to communicate."

"Stop! Please!" Buki cried, pushing Shu Mei away with her free arm.

The laser and the durian. It was too potent a mix for her senses and now the talk of ghosts? Her mind drifted back to a sleepover at twelve years old where five girls in flannel nightgowns had tried every trick they knew to wake the dead. It was Buki who could not stop giggling when they stood in front of a bathroom mirror with a candle looking for Bloody Mary or tried to summon Candyman in the hope he would appear, ready to sever them with his hook. It was Buki who sent one freckled girl into a tearful meltdown by pushing the glass on the Ouija board and keeping quiet. No, she was not superstitious. She was pragmatic, unsentimental. Give her a problem and she would find a way around it. That was what she did for a living. Working as a television producer on reality shows like *Good Girls Gone Wild* and *Asia's Secret Bulimics* was as much about putting out fires as it was creativity. She organised schedules and budgets. She managed egos and eccentricities. She fixed things. She did not swoon over stories of ghosts and goblins.

"Are you okay? Do you want some water?" asked Shu Mei.

"I'm fine. It's just … I heard a couple of weeks ago. David died."

"The ex? How?"

"A freak accident. He was sailing with some friends on a yacht off the coast of Langkawi. Apparently he dived into the water and thought he'd hit his leg on a rock. But it was some killer jellyfish. He died five hours later."

"Wa lau!"

Buki had cried when she heard and Paul, her sweet, kind, dependable fiancé was understandably confused. After all he had been the one to pick her up and dust her off when David had kicked her away, as casually as one would a pebble on a path. No matter that she had quit her job in London and moved here to be with David. His dependent. A year of smiling at compliments lined with a razor's edge. *You look nice, how much did that cost me.* Searching for work and being told she wasn't trying hard enough. *You're too nice, Buki. That's why you don't have any drive.* It had been dizzying, the speed at which he had spun away from her and even now she cringed at how small and diminished she must have looked from where he soared. The only thing that stopped her from slumping into a catatonic state when he left was that she finally found a job. A good one too, courtesy of one of the new random friends she had made while running in Fort Canning Park, a Venezuelan greeting-card artist whose neighbour co-owned a production house.

How to explain that her tears were not for the loss of the man

85

who had abandoned her on the other side of the world. They were for herself. For the apology she was never going to get nor the vindication she knew she deserved. Mostly for the youthful folly that saw her carrying the name of a dead lover on her body. It was like hoisting her very own ghost around, whose rattling chains clanged in her head at all times. So here she was, trying to fix another problem. To erase him so completely from her body that it would be as if the whole miserable episode had never happened.

"How do you talk to your Ah Ma now she's a ghost?"

"I don't."

"I thought you said she was trying to communicate."

"She makes a lot of noise, that's all. She can't do anything. Not yet. But I'll have to be ready for her in August."

"Why August?"

"How long have you lived in Singapore? The seventh month of the lunar calendar? That's when the hungry ghosts walk among us."

Buki laughed. "Well, they better stay away because I'm getting married in August."

Shu Mei took a sharp breath and her eyes bulged in alarm. "Noooo. You can't. An August wedding is bad luck."

"I don't believe in that either."

Shu Mei shook her head. "It's really not advisable to get married in Hungry Ghost Month. Or move into a new place. Or linger in swimming pools."

Buki rolled her eyes, but the hairs on the back of her neck were hard as iron filings. Little wonder that it had been so easy to find venues, even at such short notice. And with less than three months to the wedding, there could be no changes now. She sat back in the chair, and offered up her arm to Shu Mei, whose face was wreathed in concern.

* * *

After work, Buki and Paul crossed the boat-shaped Alkaff Bridge to Robertson Quay. They walked hand in hand alongside the after-work revellers, runners and cyclists, the occasional harangued mother chasing a toddler on a scooter. At their favourite Italian restaurant, they slipped behind a table, its white tablecloth ruffled by the swirling breeze. They sat side by side, thigh to thigh. She liked to look at him from this position, taking in the five o'clock shadow, the bobbing of his Adam's apple when he spoke. Paul signalled for a waiter to take their drinks order, placed a hand on her thigh. Her tattoo began to itch and the unwanted thoughts that she had swept under the carpet of her mind resurfaced.

"I've been thinking."

"About what?" His head was bent, eyes scanning the menu.

"About the wedding."

"Are you hungry? Fancy some pasta? Or maybe some fish. That would be the healthy option right?"

"You're not listening."

"I am," he said brightly, looking up. When he smiled, his face lit up like a lamp, open, exuding warmth. "You said you were thinking about something."

"No. I said ..."

The waiter arrived with a bottle of Sauvignon Blanc and a jug of water. He made quite the performance of filling their glasses and unfolding their napkins. Buki tapped her right foot on the ground until he left.

"You're a little wound up tonight, aren't you," Paul said, kneading imaginary knots from her thigh. "What happened?"

"I was thinking of the wedding and ..." Now that she had his full attention something inside her shifted, as if a tap had twisted open and she could feel her resolve trickling away. "I thought, maybe, we could postpone it a little," she said with false cheer.

Paul lifted his hand from her body and used it to close the menu, flicking the pages one by one. Their thighs were still pressed close together but now she felt his body stiffen beside her.

"What do you mean by a little?"

"I don't know, a few weeks or months."

She watched his face intently, the internal struggle to process what he heard. She imagined one of those old-fashioned data processors behind his eyes, with a myriad blinking lights and sensors bleeping, poised to overload.

"It's not that I don't want to get married," she continued. "I do. More than anything. It's just ... Did you know that August is Hungry Ghost Month in Singapore?"

"No."

"Well, apparently it's bad luck to get married in August."

He nodded and for a moment she was elated. He understood. That was what she loved about him. The opposite of David. No drama. No judgment. Even when he first saw her step out of the shower and saw her arm, the image did not bother him. "We've all got a past," he had said. "I'm only interested in the present." But now she had gone and bought that dress. Strapless, with embroidered detail at the bust and hem. She knew it was the one as soon as she tried it on and the sales assistant had oohed and aahed, said she looked like an angel. *A fallen one,* Buki thought when she looked at herself from the side. She felt sullied, wanted to wipe herself clean. That would be her gift to him.

Paul closed his eyes. When he opened them, he looked different, as if something opaque had been pulled down over the lamp and the light gone out of his face.

"You know I don't believe in ghosts," she said with a nervous laugh. "But I just thought … after … David …"

She could not finish the sentence. It had sounded ridiculous in her head and even more so once uttered. Ever since David, she had become prone to these sudden bouts of self-doubt, like radio static buzzing in her mind. She should have left well enough alone. Yet the thought of saying nothing filled her with a queasy panic.

"You could tell the truth, you know. Say you're having second thoughts."

Paul's voice was a knife twisting her gut. She was not having second thoughts. Far from it. She wanted nothing in this new relationship to remind her of the old. And yet even that was only half the truth, a denial of the many years before Singapore when she and David had been as intertwined as the vines on her tattoo. It pained her that this stable and secure second love should lack something that had been in such abundance in the first, the ability to give without holding anything back. David had taken something from her that was pure and unspoilt and now she had lost her bearings, the capacity to trust herself completely. Paul deserved that. They both did. But she had been branded in more ways than one.

"I'm not having second thoughts. I know it sounds crazy but …"

"I knew you were going to bring him up. I thought you were over all that, that you were finally ready to live in the present, but judging by your reaction when he died, you're not."

"Paul, forget I said anything."

"Stop."

"No, really, I mean it. I'm being ridiculous. Everything's paid for, we'd lose all the money. It's not even a viable suggestion."

"I'd rather lose the money than walk down the aisle with someone whose heart isn't really in it." He sighed, wiped a hand across his forehead. "I'm tired and seem to have lost my appetite."

Paul picked at his meal, while Buki, suddenly famished, wolfed down hers. When he stood up to pay the bill, she thought again about how different he was from the man whose name was stamped on her skin. Even now, when hurt and disappointed, he did not project his anger. She turned to face the river, squinting at the lights bouncing on the water's surface. He signalled to leave and she slipped a trembling hand into his outstretched palm.

* * *

It was Shu Mei's idea for Buki to accompany her to Punggol Beach. Earlier in the day, Shu-Mei had visited the temple in Yishun with a plate of steamed buns and braised duck – her grandmother's favourite dish. Buki was surprised to discover that Shu Mei's Ah Ma was far from a doting grandmother. Instead, she had been moody and cranky, a disgruntled soul who had emigrated reluctantly to Singapore from China and never let a day go past without voicing her displeasure with the smallness of her new life.

"Did you get along with her?"

"About as well as you would get on with a scorpion. I learnt to keep my distance."

"So why do you think she's haunting you?"

Shu Mei shrugged. "I think I was her favourite. At least, her favourite to torture. She was always lamenting about my hair and my teeth and my skin."

Buki cast a sideways look at her friend, the mini craters lodged on her friend's face. She had never given any thought to what it must be like for Shu Mei, helping others to clear up their blemishes, and yet unable to help herself.

"If she was such a dragon, why make offerings to her?"

"Not just her. All the ancestors. They are ravenous when they leave hell. Besides, if she eats well, then maybe she'll leave my apartment and find someone else to torment."

They timed it just right, arriving by taxi as the last of the day's rays were melting into night. The water lapped gently against the shore, and they tasted the salt spray in the air. They walked along the promenade, finally coming to a deserted stretch of beach. They removed their shoes, rolled their trousers up to the knees and picked a path among rocks and boulders to reach the water's edge. The sand was wet and dense, cool beneath their feet. Shu Mei had bought some paper lanterns. Buki watched her friend intently, following each of her steps, unwrapping the lantern carefully, lighting a candle with a lighter she bought from the 7-Eleven, placing it in the centre, surrounded by a circle of lotus blossoms. Buki stepped into the water, just ankle deep, marvelling for a moment at the sensation of the ebbing water pulling at the sand under her feet. She took a few more steps, crouched down and placed the offering onto the water.

She had not seen David for years and for a time she had wished all manner of tortures for him. But she would never have wanted this. Paul had offered to join her, but she was glad to come alone. It had never seemed right to grieve for David, not in front of Paul, but she could say goodbye now. To their former selves. So young when they first got together, so sure what they felt would never end. It had been a rare and delicate thing for a time, like those papyrus scrolls discovered in Ancient Egypt. They lasted centuries in dry climates but disintegrated in humid conditions. Some things were just not made for the tropics.

"Help the spirits find their way back to hell," Shu Mei said gently.

Buki stood up, watching as the lantern bobbed away, the candle still flickering, waiting for the light to go out.

* * *

The morning of her final laser appointment, Buki looked in the mirror, horrified. Some people got lucky. Some people spent $1500 and got what they paid for. Clearly she was not one of those people. She pulled at the flesh of her arm, peering at her reflection. The lovers' heads were decapitated, the vines still vivid, the bodies and the printed words had faded to a dirty smudge. She turned away from the mirror in disgust, replaying the conversation she had shared with Paul the night before. "Nothing that a little make-up can't fix," he had said.

Buki dressed hurriedly, deciding to kill a few hours in Bugis. The mall was yet to come alive, only a handful of stores open for business, so she browsed shop windows, staring absently at a stand of cheap necklaces one moment, a rack of shoes the next. Traffic noises seeped into the relative quiet of the mall. She watched a pigeon fly in through some automatic doors, then circle the air looking for a way out. A group of young tourists with tie-dye dresses and dreadlocks walked past carrying coffee cups. Maybe that was what she needed. Maybe that would bring relief. She trudged along in the direction from which the girls had come. Rounding a corner, she spotted artwork in a shopfront window and walked through the open door. The exposed brick walls inside were lined with boxes stuffed with prints, the biggest of which were mounted above.

A voice from behind startled her. "Interesting image you've got there."

A man gestured to her arm with his head. He had gelled black hair with a side parting and his shirt-sleeves were rolled up. A smaller version of a design gracing the walls was etched onto his arm. Only then did she notice the chair in the corner of the room. She guessed that this space doubled as a tattoo parlour.

"Well, that's one way of putting it."

"Looks like ghosting to me," he said.

Buki looked at him, perplexed. Not another person worried about hungry demons.

"When you're left with an outline of the original image," he explained while moving boxes around, rearranging the layout of the store. "So are you here for a cover up?"

"God, no! Sorry. No offence but I'm done with tattoos. I've been trying to laser this one off and look at it."

"Sure. I get it. Bad breakup."

"Is it that obvious?"

He smiled in answer. She moved over to one of the new boxes, sifting through its contents.

"Do you design all these yourself?" Buki asked

"Most."

She thought the designs were beautiful, some breath-taking even. She had a sudden memory of the day she had had the first tattoo. She had been terrified of course, though not of making a mistake. There had been none of that "What will I look like in thirty years" self-questioning because of course she and David would still be together in thirty years! Her biggest fear was not being able to handle the pain. It did hurt but it had been worth it. It had been therapeutic to translate all her feelings, all that swirling emotion into ink on her body. How empowering it felt to create something visible and irreversible, and not be afraid of what anyone would think. When did that change? When had she learnt to put herself in a cage? Buki looked up to find the man still looking at her arm.

"Would you ever add to something like this?" she asked.

"Yeah," he said. "Think of it this way. Whether you add to it or cover it, you change it. You make it new."

"Sort of like the first time."

"Maybe even better."

Buki cocked her head to the side, pondering what he said.

"Do you mind?" he asked and lifted her arm, guiding her towards the mirror on the wall. He began drawing invisible lines that flowed out of the mess left behind, his voice exuberant. "We could expand the vines so it's more Gothic. Or go geometric and make it bigger. Or bring these lines together and draw a circle round them, sort of like a ..."

"A compass!"

"Sure, why not, a compass. In fact, now that you bring it up …"

He dropped her arm and pulled out a manila file from behind the counter. Inside were postcard-size drawings, freshly inked. "Something I've been working on. We could change things a bit, create a little space, but I think it would work."

Buki felt something give way, a tightness dissolve deep in her gut. "How long will it take?"

"How long do you have?"

"I'm getting married in two weeks!"

"I was actually talking about how much time you have now."

They both laughed. He could be finished within four hours, he said. Her skin would need four weeks to heal but the image would look good in two. He was giving her a lecture on aftercare but Buki barely listened. She dropped her handbag on the floor and slid into the chair.

"Alright!" he said.

While he rummaged in the storeroom, she held up the card, stared at the image. Then she picked up her mobile phone and texted Paul, asking him to meet her here. It would be different this time. She knew that. This was all about her, but she wanted to share the moment with him somehow. The tattoo artist returned with a tray of inks. Buki leaned back, watching as he prepared the stencil. She was ready for the needle that would bite into her skin, tracing a path true north. She was ready to savour the pain.

About the Author
Shola Olowu-Asante is a writer and journalist. In 2010, her story, "Dinner for Three", was one of the winners in the Commonwealth Short Story Competition. She has an MA in Creative Writing from Lancaster University and her short fiction has been published in *Cleaver Magazine*, *The Linnet's Wings* and various anthologies of stories from around the globe.

THE THINGS WE HIDE

CLARISSA N. GOENAWAN

I flip the calendar from November to December. The page is decorated with a photograph of cascading waterfalls.

"It's finally that time of year, huh?" the woman says.

"Go away!" I shoo her, but she ignores me.

In 2009, December 19th will fall on Saturday. That day comes and goes every year, no matter what I do. But unlike December 19th, my boyfriend came into my life, left, and never returned.

* * *

My boyfriend was eight years older. We'd met at work.

He was a senior editor at a publishing firm, and I was one of the freelance editors. My job only paid minimum wage, barely enough to cover my son's half-day childcare fee and our day-to-day expenses.

"I didn't know you had a baby," he said, when he turned up at my flat to pick up a manuscript.

I nodded, my son in my arms. My hair was messy, and I didn't wear any make-up. Usually it was the company's driver who did the collection. I didn't expect the senior editor to come.

"So cute." He touched my son's cheek. "What's the baby's name?"

"Chenxi," I answered. "He just turned ten months old yesterday."

"He's big for his age, isn't he? Such a handsome boy." He smiled at me. "I was under the impression that you were single. Maybe because you're still so young."

"I am." I forced myself to laugh. "I'm still single. Not yet married."

"Oh." That was his only reaction.

He smiled awkwardly and left in a hurry. I felt slightly hurt. I must have made a bad impression.

But a few weeks later, he asked me out for dinner. Without hesitation, I said yes and asked my mother to babysit Chenxi. I wore the classiest dress I had, a black wrap dress I'd bought during a sale. I tied up my hair and wore red lipstick. To complete the look, I put on a pair of silver high heels.

When I took out the shoebox, it was covered with a thick film of dust. When was the last time I'd taken them out? I guess it was one of the things that change once you have a baby.

We went to a French restaurant at Dempsey. The place was too fancy for my liking. I couldn't pronounce most of the words on the menu. He, on the other hand, looked completely at ease.

"I come here often," he said.

After a five-course meal and two glasses of wine, he drove me back in his black sedan. On the stretch of Orchard Road, surrounded by the glittering streetlights, he asked me if I'd consider spending more time together. And I agreed.

* * *

I drag a cardboard box from the storeroom to the living room. It's not that heavy, but I'm out of breath. Guess I'm getting old. Thirty-nine and single, how depressing. Pressing my key into the cello tape that secures the box, I cut a straight line. An image of a descending plane flashes into my mind. I shake my head. Not again. It was over.

I take out a folded white shirt from the box. There are two more shirts inside, a striped powder blue one and another in plain grey. A few pieces of underwear and some socks. Those are the clothes my boyfriend left behind. Underneath, there is a notebook. I flip through it aimlessly.

SilkAir Flight 185: Controversial Crash. The Pilot Who Wanted To Die. Grieving Relatives Recall SilkAir Crash Victims. Insufficient Evidence of Murder. Experts Still Divided on SilkAir Murder-Suicide Theory. The articles I collected over the years fill up two-thirds of the notebook.

"Does it matter whether it was a murder-suicide or not?" the woman asks.

"Probably only to the family of the pilot," I answer. No matter what happened, the fact that he perished in that flight will never change. "By any chance, are you one of the plane crash victims?"

She tilts her head.

"It just occurred to me," I say.

"If that's the case, isn't it strange that it was me who appeared to you instead of him?" She leans toward me. "Maybe he never cared about you."

I clench my fist. How could she be so insensitive? One thing

I'm certain of, she's a wandering spirit. Once a living, breathing human being, but for some reason, her soul can't rest. And maybe, just maybe …

"Do you think you can talk to my boyfriend?"

She shrugs and walks away.

"Can you ask him to visit me?" I follow her. "Once is enough. Please, I'm begging you."

She turns around. "It doesn't work that way."

"Then what should I do?"

She doesn't answer.

"Fine, suit yourself."

I close the notebook and put it on top of the clothes. Tucked into the corner of the box, I find some pens, post-it notes, and a box of paperclips. My boyfriend used to bring his work to my place. And what else is there? A box of expired condoms, of course. I take it out and throw it away.

"You should've gotten rid of all of his stuff," the woman says.

She knows I can't do that. If I did, I wouldn't have anything concrete to remember him by.

"Get over it. The man died long time ago. It's been twelve years."

I ignore her and seal the box, dragging it back to the storeroom.

She peers over my shoulder. "Are you going to Changi Airport again?"

"I am." I slide the box into the lowest rack. "You don't need to come with me if you don't want to."

"I haven't said that. Don't put words in my mouth."

She disappears with a sinister laugh.

That woman, she gets on my nerves. She appeared around the same time my boyfriend had gone. The first time I saw her, I thought she was a thief who broke into my apartment. But when I tried to chase her out, I'd the shock of my life when everything I threw at her went through. For the first few weeks, I'd been afraid and pretended she didn't exist. Seeing things other people don't is never a good sign.

After a while, I got used to it. She appeared more often, and we started to talk. Or rather, argue. Yet, when I'm alone, her presence becomes an odd comfort. After my boyfriend disappeared, I was lonely.

"He didn't disappear. He died."

There she is, appearing and disappearing as she pleases.

"I know. You don't need to tell me."

"But you haven't accepted his death. You're still waiting."

I keep quiet. Deep down, I know she's right. I can't believe he's dead. And I'm still hoping that one day, he'll return to me.

* * *

My boyfriend called me from Jakarta the night before he disappeared. Things were tense between us. We'd been arguing frequently. Sometimes we could go for weeks without talking until one of us eventually apologised. More often than not, it was me who did. After that, things went back to normal, but only for a while. We couldn't shake the fact that we were both at our wits' end. This relationship was draining us.

"Why didn't you pick up my call?" I asked, sitting on my bed. I'd tried to sleep but couldn't.

"I had back-to-back meetings," he answered. "My cell phone was on silent."

"But I've been calling you since this morning. You should've noticed my missed calls." I glanced at the alarm clock on my bedside table. "What took you so long to return my call? It's already past eleven."

"I was busy. I just arrived in my hotel room a few minutes ago."

I could sense that he was getting irritated.

"I'm sorry," I quickly said.

"It's okay." His voice softened. The sound of the shower ran in the background. "Anyway, why did you call me? Didn't I tell you not to call when I'm overseas?"

I cleared my throat. "I've got something important to discuss."

"Did anything happen?"

I paused for a moment. "I'd like to talk about it in person."

"Then you should've waited until I return."

"I'm sorry." Again, I apologised. Not because I was at fault, but because I didn't want to get into another argument. "What time will you be back tomorrow? Can you come over to my place?"

"I should be back in the evening." He paused. "But it's not a good time. Christmas is coming so I've got plenty of family matters to attend to. I can only see you next year."

Whenever he told me he was busy, I felt a sharp pain in my chest. Was that jealousy? Or insecurity? Probably a bit of both.

"I don't want to wait until next year," I insisted.

He sighed. "Fine, I'll check my schedule once I'm in Singapore. But don't call me. I'll call you. You'll hear from me by tomorrow, or the day after tomorrow at the latest. I promise."

"All right." I laid down on the bed. "I miss you."

"Me too," he said. "Now go to sleep. It's already late."

"Uh-huh."

He hung up and I put my phone down back on top of the bedside table. And that was the last conversation I had with him. My boyfriend didn't keep his promise. He never called back.

* * *

I knock on the door, but there's no response.

"Chenxi ..." I call and knock again.

"What?" he shouted.

I turn the doorknob and opened the door. My son sits in front of the computer. Right hand on the mouse, left hand on the keyboard. His eyes are glued to the monitor.

"I'm going to be home late today," I say. "It's for work."

"Okay." He doesn't even look at me.

"What about your dinner? Do you want me to cook something?"

"No need. I'll eat out." He finally turned to me. "Mum, are you done? You're breaking my concentration."

"I'll leave some money under the TV remote."

I close the door quietly. The woman appears when I'm looking for my wallet.

"Don't take it personally," she says. "Most teenagers ignore their parents. It doesn't mean that you're a bad mother."

What she said should have been comforting, but I don't want to hear it from her. It sounds as if she's mocking me.

* * *

After the plane crash, I stopped travelling by air. If I wanted to go for a short getaway with Chenxi, I would either take a bus or a ferry. Because of that, our holiday options were limited to Malaysia and Indonesia. Once, when Chenxi was six, he'd asked why we never took a plane.

"My friend said it's faster," he said when I was helping him to get ready for school. "You can reach Kuala Lumpur in an hour."

"I'm afraid of heights."

"It's okay, Mum." He tugged my sleeve. "We're going together. You've got nothing to be afraid of."

I smiled and felt proud.

"He's right, you know." The woman appeared next to Chenxi. "You've got nothing to be afraid of."

I glared at her. She wasn't supposed to talk to me when my son was around.

"Don't be so mean." She rolled her eyes. "The boy can't see me."

I wished I could find a way to get rid of her.

"Stop it! He'll think you're crazy if you keep staring at me like that." She laughed and wore a smug smile. "You don't think it's funny?"

I ignored her and helped my son put his shoes on.

"Do you really want to take a plane?" I asked Chenxi.

"I think it would be fun." His face lit up. "Can we do that on the next school holiday?"

"I'll see what I can do." I passed him his water bottle. "But no promises. I don't want you to be disappointed."

"Uh-huh." He picked up his backpack. "I'm leaving."

"Take care." I gave him a hug and watched him as he walked into the elevator. His bag was so big that I couldn't see his neck.

* * *

When was the last time I hugged Chenxi? Was it when he went to primary school? Or was it earlier? I couldn't recall. Recently he's been avoiding my embraces, dismissing them as if they're embarrassing. When he was a baby, I used to wish for him to grow up quickly so I could take a break. But now, I miss those early days when he always yearned for me.

"It's always the case, isn't it?"

I open my eyes. That woman sits opposite me. The train carriage is almost empty, save for a small number of passengers. Three Caucasians with big luggage, most likely tourists. Two youngsters who look like they're looking for an air-conditioned place to study overnight. The train, waiting for more passengers to board, has not moved from Tanah Merah Station.

"You never realise how important a person is until they're no longer around," she continues. "You're full of regret, and you're trapped in the past."

Rubbish. She's wrong about me.

"Is that so? Then why do you go to the airport every year on the anniversary of his death?"

Shut up and go away.

"But if I leave, you'll have no one who knows what you've been going through." She stands and holds the silver pole. She bends at the waist until her face is just a few centimetres away from mine. "Admit it. You need me."

The loudspeaker makes an announcement that the doors are closing. A number of commuters make their last-minute dash.

I clench my fists and say what I should've said long time ago. "I don't need you. Because soon, I'm going to meet him, and we'll finish what we started."

"Oh! What makes you so sure?"

"Because he promised."

The doors close and the train starts to move. The woman's outline is getting blurred, and soon, she disappears with a proud smile on her lips.

* * *

My cell phone is buzzing. It's the alarm. I take it out from my handbag to turn it off. The time reads 4:19 PM. The plane that my boyfriend was in took a nosedive into the Musi River at this exact time.

I look around the airport. From the corner of my eye, I see that woman standing a few metres behind. She looks at me, and our eyes meet. I quickly turn away and walk off, but she comes over.

"Stop following me," I say. "Leave me alone."

"Fine, if that's what you want."

She stops walking and slowly fades away, leaving me stunned. It's the first time she's ever listened to me. Not that I care. I hope she's gone for good.

The sun shines through the glass panels, casting a yellowish hue on the spotless tiles. A blistering hot afternoon. That fateful day, the weather was exactly like this. I remember showering Chenxi inside our cramped bathroom.

* * *

"I don't like to shower," he complained.

I ignored him and continued to rub his legs with the foaming sponge. It was humid, and the lukewarm water had made it worse. I wiped the sweat off my forehead with the back of my hand.

Ironic, wasn't it? To sweat profusely inside a bathroom.

I felt a splash of water on my face. Chenxi had put his hands under the running tap water and squeezed it to create bubbles.

"Stop it." I turned off the tap. "I'm getting wet."

He burst into laughter, and I tried hard to suppress mine.

Did I feel something was amiss then? No, I didn't. Neither sixth sense nor woman's instinct, whatever people call it. To me, it was just another hot day. I only realised something was amiss when I read the morning newspaper the day after.

The plane crash was all over the headlines, and I found my boyfriend's name among the list of the victims. I couldn't believe what I saw, so I rang his office. My call was automatically transferred to another editor.

"Yes," his colleague said in a heavy voice. "I'm afraid it was really him."

I hung up without saying a word. I dropped on the floor and began to cry. I was so distraught that I didn't notice Chenxi had returned from school.

"Mum." He peered over at me. "Are you alright?"

I looked at him in a daze.

"I'm hungry."

"Ah …" I stood up and hastily cooked his lunch, fried rice and poached egg. My body moved automatically even though I couldn't think clearly. It was probably my inner defence system. Regardless, I managed to get through the day.

After I tucked my son in bed, I calmed myself and went through the news. The experts were divided on what had actually happened. Good weather, experienced crew, a relatively new aircraft, and no distress signals prior to the crash. There were too many unanswered questions, but none of them mattered. I only wanted my boyfriend to return.

* * *

Opening my eyes, I found myself in an unfamiliar room. It's dark. All the curtains are drawn. The single source of light comes from the bathroom, where the door has been left ajar.

"Did I wake you up?"

My boyfriend sits on the couch, a cigarette in his hand, wearing only his boxers.

"What time is it?" I ask.

He reaches for his cell phone and presses a button. The yellowish light from the screen highlights his face. "It's almost three."

"What time do you need to go?"

"Probably soon." He crushes his cigarette on the ashtray, before climbing into the bed and sitting next to me. "Come here."

I move closer and lay my head against his chest. Neither of us says much. The faint rumble from the air conditioner is audible. My boyfriend kisses my forehead and rubs my hair. I feel so comfortable, but then I remember, he's supposed to be dead.

"This is a dream, isn't it?" I break the silence.

He whispers, "And what if it is?"

"It doesn't matter if it's a dream, as long as we're together."

"Really?"

I nod. "I've been wanting to see you."

"Me too." He reaches for my hand and doesn't let go. "I took really long to get back to you, didn't I? I promised to call in two days, but look at me now."

He's frustrated, I can tell. He's angry he had to die so early. His life was cut short abruptly and he wasn't ready.

"Why only now can you come and see me?" I ask.

"I'm not so sure also. Perhaps because it's been a twelve-year Chinese zodiac cycle?" He looks at me. "Anyway, it's no longer important. Now that we can finally see each other, tell me, what did you want to talk about?"

I hesitate before saying. "I was pregnant."

"Ah." He jerks a little and releases my hand. "You were …"

"Pregnant, yes. I was pregnant, but I aborted it." I slip away from his embrace and sit facing him. "I'm sorry I made the decision without consulting you. But after Chenxi, I didn't want to raise another child alone, and you were no longer around."

"I understand." He pulls me back into his arms. "It's my fault for being careless. I feel bad I couldn't be there when you needed me the most."

I look at him but can't make out his expression.

He holds me tighter. "I'm so sorry, Yuen."

Once he stops talking, the silence envelopes us once more.

I press my left ear to his chest. I try to catch his heartbeat, but I hear nothing. He's no longer living in the same world as I am, and thinking about it hurts me so much.

"How was the funeral?" he asks.

"I don't know." I shrug. "I didn't go."

He laughs. "You didn't miss much. At most, all you would have seen was an old photograph of me and an empty casket."

"And your family. Your wife and your children. They wouldn't have liked to see me."

He hugs me tighter. I close my eyes and breathe in his fragrance. He smells nice, probably from his aftershave.

"That woman," my boyfriend says. "Is she bothering you?"

"She's all bent on making me angry."

"Don't worry. After today, she won't be bothering you."

"Was she someone you knew?"

He doesn't answer.

"Is she the junior editor you were working with?"

He looks surprised. "Did she tell you that?"

"No, but one of your colleagues told me about the gossip."

He sighs. "So people knew."

"Was she on the plane too?"

Again, no reply.

"Why did she come to me?"

"I don't know. I wasn't even aware that she did, until today."

I glance at my boyfriend. He's beside me, but he feels so distant. Always.

"Yuen, I heard that you're still holding on to the things I left at your place," he says. "I appreciate you're taking good care of them. But please, throw them away. They're holding you back."

I ignore him. "Is it possible for us to stay here forever? I don't want to be separated from you again."

"I wish I could say yes, but that's not possible. The dead are dead, and the living should go on living. That's the rule, isn't it?" He pauses. "Your time has not come yet. I can't take you now, even if I wanted to."

* * *

I wake up feeling cold. I've fallen asleep on a bench in Terminal 2, and the pashmina shawl I wore has slipped off. I pick it up and wrap it around my shoulders before checking my watch. Four in the morning. It feels as if I've just slept for a little while, but more than six hours have passed.

Recalling what my boyfriend told me about that woman, I look around for her. He was right. I can't find any trace of her.

"Are you still here? Or have you gone for real?"

No answer. She's no longer with me. I can sense it.

Actually, I finally understand why she has been following me. She was probably worried about me. We were in the same position, longing for someone we couldn't have. For all it was worth, I could have been her, and she could have been me. Now that I've come to this understanding, I'm a little sad that she's gone, but I also feel relieved.

Once I get the burden off my chest, I start to feel hungry. At this hour, the only choices I have are fast food. Burger King or McDonalds? It doesn't matter, either one is fine. I'll go to the less crowded one. I make a mental note: After I eat, I'll take the first train home and prepare a nice breakfast for Chenxi. And after that, I'll get rid of that box.

About the Author

Clarissa N. Goenawan loves rainy days, pretty books, and hot green tea. Her first novel, *Rainbirds*, is the winner of the 2015 Bath Novel Award. Her short stories have won several awards and been published in various literary magazines and anthologies.

A different version of "The Things We Hide" was previously published in *Black Denim Lit* (Dec 2014).

THE GARDENER

RAELEE CHAPMAN

The egg did not belong in the nest. Rakesh knew this because the koel egg was different, ruddy, flecked; it rested among the lacquered sea-green eggs of a crow. The koel mother had simply tipped one egg out and replaced it with her own.

How happy he was to find the egg here in Singapore, the koel being the state bird of his hometown. Often heard but rarely seen, they were his alarm clock here as in India. He would tell Neeta about the egg later when he called her. She'd like that. He began pruning the trees that bordered the condominium driveway from the canal, struggling with the garden shears on the ladder. Rakesh was pleased he'd been given the shears today, he preferred the shade. On the ground lay the sad, smashed shell of the discarded egg. Ants marched through a stream of spilt yolk. He was not surprised, he had always known the elusive songbirds were cunning.

Waxy leaves brushed against his beard as he climbed higher. He tilted his head back to watch a plane move directly above him, blotting out the sun. The engine rumble was so loud he almost lost his footing on the ladder. It had only been thirty days since Rakesh took his first flight. He spent most of the journey white-knuckled, heavy with sweat, gripping his tray-table or in the restroom sluicing water over this face. How did five hundred tonnes of steel stay up in the air like that?

His brother Sunil, a good-for-nothing drunk and gambler had pushed him to it. A new agency had set up back home. Sunil as eldest son said his place was with their mother but that Rakesh should go. It all happened so fast. He was able-bodied, clear of infectious diseases, young, fit – they needed him. Agencies were sending men to Singapore to earn Sing dollars! He didn't even need to buy his air ticket; it would later be deducted from his salary. Back home, he and Neeta slumbered in a single room with Sunil, his sister-in-law, his nephew Ajith, and his mother. Sunil spent any money he had, leaving Rakesh to support everyone else. His mother, going blind, spent her days praying at the temple; they had no money to scrape the cataracts from her eyes. Now Neeta was pregnant, there were more expenses to cover. Singapore was a fresh start for Rakesh, a place where he could earn big money. Where nobody cared about his caste or the unfortunate accident at the jam factory where he last worked.

The factory had been a shadowy building; the only light came from the jaundiced glow of low-watt bulbs overhead. In the unsettling light, the jams looked like congealed blood. But here, he worked outdoors. The condo was freshly painted and its exteriors shone in an ivory blaze. Several of his co-workers were dotted around the garden beds on either side of the drive, their faces mummified in Good Morning tea towels, ripping up weeds or snipping at sunburnt plants, just the way Mr Lim, the condo manager, liked.

"Must look tidy. Cut all away from driveway. Monsoon come cannot have branches dropping down on people's Mercedes,"

Mr Lim had instructed him earlier in person as the foreman was off sick.

"Yes, sir," Rakesh gave a nod to each rapid-fire instruction.

"Trim it all back ... everything. That bird nest must destroy also. Disturb the residents, lah. You also don't disturb, okay. Don't go close to people's apartments," Mr Lim added before walking away.

The shears were dotted in rust and in need of oil. Rakesh, not good with his hands, was unwieldy in his effort to trim the thicker branches.

Neeta was excellent with her hands. He thought of the way those lovely brown fingers would knead chapattis, slamming small mounds on a wooden board, sending clouds of flour into her face. The way she swiftly did her hair, parting it in three, weaving an inverted plait she called a fishtail. He would watch her wrap sweets in the evening on the floor of their hut. A mound of rainbow fruit jelly that he lugged from the jam factory lay at her feet. They got a small sum for each sack of sweets she wrapped.

Thinking about the jelly made him hungry though it was still early. The morning sun seared as it rose. His long-sleeved green shirt was already drenched with sweat. The grounds were quiet and the only noises came from the bordering canal. Occasionally a slight breeze blew and he could smell stagnant storm water. A small pile of branches fell to the ground as he cut away an aperture, which gave him a good view across the driveway into a ground floor unit. The lace day curtains were open. A child's playmat with candy-cane striped arches lay on the floor. A marbled grey couch lined one wall and a large flat-screen TV was flickering. A young Caucasian couple lived there with a new baby. He'd seen the baby, pink and hairless in its mother's arms as she strolled around the condo. Elderly Chinese men with sweatbands and bamboo sticks powered along the path outside, chanting vocal breath exercises as they went. Rakesh listened to their, "Oooh Ahh Hum," as he tried to make out the hanging felt animals on the playmat. He would tell Neeta; perhaps she could sew some just like that.

Rakesh returned to lopping a thick branch as a dog bounded down the drive without a lead, a tall man jogged beside it, heading for the canal. Rakesh scrambled up a rung or two higher. He hated dogs. Even the sight of them caused a gnawing pain in his stomach. The memory of sixteen injections in the abdomen after a deranged dog bit him at a cricket game. He'd been staring at the sky waiting for the ball to drop into his hands. The dog also wanted the ball. Neeta had been there, seen it happen. They were teenagers then. She'd rushed over to stop him making a mud compress for the wound saying, "No, water is better." She made him go to a clinic. Get the shots. His stomach had swelled up hard like a pomegranate. He'd got lucky that time. "No rabies in Singapore," Neeta told him before he left for Chennai to get the plane to Changi. She had been standing at the train station, crying rivers of kohl, her red kurta straining against her swollen belly.

From the canal, a bicycle bell pealed and a flock of pigeons scattered, their grey-purple tinged wings beat in the clammy air. Rakesh realised he'd been doing nothing, daydreaming again. His arms rested, slumped over a rung of the ladder. Lucky Mr Lim was not around. "Daydreaming causes accidents," Neeta always said. Just like the last time, he thought, as he examined his hands.

His livelihood, intact, unharmed. His cousin Kommaluri, at the factory, was not so lucky. The thick, sweet smell of jam had made Rakesh dizzy, swirls of dust motes in the factory air made him wonder if he was actually breathing in sugar. He had let a pile of labels slip into the labelling machine. Kommaluri was quick to retrieve them and lost two fingers in the process. It was impossible to work there after that. Marring his mother's brother's son, a blood relative that lived two doors down. There was no end to the shame. Rakesh would go to the factory only once a week to collect the sack of jelly for Neeta and returned with it, wearied as though it were lead.

Rakesh arched his back a little, feeling the sweat run in rivulets down his spine and shook off that memory. He cut a larger viewing hole amongst the branches, confused by Mr Lim's instructions. He was no longer sure if the trees were a border to stop people from outside looking in or whether he should actually give residents a view of the canal and the pocket of jungle beyond. The glare reflecting off the buildings now hurt his eyes and he was thirsty.

"Rakesh, that tree is a mess already. Move to the next," a co-worker called up to him from across the drive.

"I nearly finish," he replied.

"Mr Lim tell you to cut it like that?" another called out. Rakesh nodded. He could hear his co-workers laugh from the garden bed. They often laughed at him. He was the newest. When the next-off-the-plane joined their work crew, Rakesh will join the others to laugh at him. That is how it was. He wouldn't tell Neeta that. These were not the things he told Neeta at night, in the dark of the dormitory when the others were grunting and passing wind in their sleep. He would tell Neeta how today, he saved a bird's nest. He reached out to touch the fragile eggs and wondered how to hide the nest from Mr Lim. The koel egg looked similar to the others but was smaller, speckled. Why couldn't the crow mother tell it apart from her own? He would ask Neeta. They looked for commonalities whenever they spoke.

She would ask, "What do you hear in this country?"

And he told her, "Every evening when I finish my shift. I hear no packs of street dogs whimpering and whining such as what we hear at home. But I hear koels roosting at dusk, the male's ku-oo, ku-oo and the female's kik kik kik as they sing to each other and get ready to sleep."

"I hear koels too. They are shy, hidden in the bael fruit trees outside, but their song is strong. We hear the same thing," Neeta replied.

When he complained about how far apart they were, her reply was always the same, "Same sky we sleep under, Rakesh." As if a blanket stretched so far and they were in fact still enveloped together.

In the ground floor unit, across the way, the mother walked into the living room, carrying the baby, which was dressed only in a diaper. Her brown hair was wet, dripping as if she had just stepped from the shower. She sat on the couch and flicked through channels with the remote, the baby in her lap. The baby reminded him of when his nephew was born. His sister-in-law, that dull ugly woman from the countryside, wouldn't hold him. A black cloud fell upon her the day Ajith was born with a harelip. Rakesh carried and jiggled his nephew, rocked him in his hammock. Neeta would water down condensed milk and bottle-feed him. Since birth,

Ajith had never lain with is parents but slept nestled into the arch of Rakesh's back, murmuring softly. He knew Neeta would make sure Ajith, who was still young, would not feel supplanted by the new baby. He said a quick prayer for blessings for his child and an uncomplicated delivery. He dropped the shears to the ground beside the ladder feeling uneasy all of a sudden. He wiped the sweat from his brow. His hand was covered with rust filaments and smelt metallic. He should say a quick prayer for Ajith, who would sleep where …? Nestled into Neeta's back, while the baby rests in her arms?

He watched the woman reposition the baby in the nook of her arm. She pulled down a strap of her singlet, exposing one creamy, full breast. The baby turned its head towards her, its little mouth opening in a wide pink O as it fish-gaped to latch on. His sister-in-law had her milk dry up, she couldn't stand the sight of Ajith's cursed little mouth, she'd said. While baby and mother melded together in the living room, Rakesh's chest seized as he pictured Neeta with their child. How could he leave her alone? His body was dissolving in sweat and tears, he thought as he swirled and spat brackish bile that rose like a tide within him. He rubbed the rust filaments into his eyes. The ladder swayed though there was no breeze. He should not have let Sunil persuade him Singapore was best. He realised his sister-in-law who did nothing to care for Ajith would have to help with the new baby. His baby. Maybe even care full time for his child while Neeta cared for Ajith. Is this why they pushed him away? He must go home. He would tell his foreman, pay back his ticket in instalments, and find a job in the next village. In his mind, these things were possible, and at that moment, quashing the hurt was not.

Then he remembered Neeta, on the platform at the train station, already thanking him for the better life he would give them. His mother, whose prayers dutifully chanted with milky downcast eyes had been answered. Her cataracts, Ajith's harelip, support for Kommaluri, Neeta's hospital fees, and delivery – little by little his money would help all. He swallowed, coughed, the ocean receding inside him; the sick feeling replaced by pride. He puffed out his chest, took a deep breath, retrieved the shears, and was ready to begin work again.

The gate to the canal clanged shut as the man he'd seen earlier returned from his jog, dragging his mutt up the driveway. Rakesh paused a moment on the ladder, waiting for the dog to pass. Mr Lim was at the foot of the drive, calling towards him, "Get down. Get down this moment! You cause big trouble. Disturb resident," he shouted. In the ground floor unit, the baby now lay on the playmat. Rakesh hadn't even realised it had finished feeding. The mother paced while she talked on her mobile phone. She waved her hands as she spoke, pointing at Rakesh, and scowling as a maid hurriedly drew the curtains. Mr Lim stormed towards him, furious. Rakesh wanted to get down but with the dog loitering near the spilt egg yolk, he couldn't let go of the ladder. Daydreaming causes accidents. He didn't know how he would explain this all to Neeta. As he turned to face Mr Lim, the shears dislodged the nest. Already before it hit the ground, he could hear the shattering of the delicate shells.

About the Author

Raelee Chapman grew up in the Riverina, Australia. Since 2011, she has lived in Singapore with her family. Her fiction and narrative non-fiction have been published in Australia and overseas, most recently in *Southerly* and *Mascara Literary Review*.

THE RUBY CASE

WAN PHING LIM

For the past half hour, Corporal Justin Kong had been staring into Roslan Ibrahim's apartment unit, with no shadow or movement coming from the open windows. The sun was to his back as he stood on Marsiling Rise, a hillock which looked straight into the fifth floor unit of the old man's flat. Justin took a last whiff of his cigarette and squashed it with his black shoe.

Roslan's wife had been missing for a week, but the old man did not seem to care. Justin had been watching him for four days now, going about his daily routine, spending long afternoons at the coffee shop, and feeding his birds – three of them, each housed in a rattan cage that hung outside his balcony window. He had an adult son, Alfi, and the young man didn't seem fazed either.

Justin rubbed his eyes and waited a little while longer. Last night he had been to see Delia and was almost late reporting to work this morning. The missing woman's case had been wearing him out, and there never seemed to be enough cigarettes to keep him occupied during the long hours of camping out at Marsiling Hill.

The week before when Justin appeared outside unit #05-06 to question Roslan, the man had been more interested in showing him his caged birds: the black-naped oriole, the *mata puteh* and his most prized possession of all, the red-whiskered bulbul, which he said could sell for up to $20,000 once it wins a few singing competitions.

His son, Alfi, was not home that day, and that was why Justin decided to pay them another visit today.

* * *

It was the cats in the Roslan household that Justin couldn't stand – four of them, climbing all over the furniture and watching him with suspicion as he scanned the room for evidence.

"Mr Roslan, when was the last time you saw your wife?" Justin asked, circling the oak wood dining table. He had asked the same question during his first visit, but he wanted to be sure that Roslan was consistent with his answers.

Roslan sat at the dining table with a glass of black tea in his hand. His placid face was etched with lines, his eyes glazed and not looking at the Corporal. Instead, they were focused outside the window as though he were waiting for someone.

"Two weeks ago, sir." When at last he spoke, his voice was weak and soft.

"Rubianah, your wife, did she tell you where she was going?"

"Yes, Ruby, my Ruby. When is she coming home?"

Justin repeated himself. "Did she tell you where she was going?"

"She went on the Hajj. To Mecca. Ruby is devoted like that." He smiled.

"And when was she supposed to be back?"

"Last week." He hit the side of his head with his palm, as

though he were shaking away a migraine.

"Last week when?"

"Tuesday. Oh no, Wednesday. Ah, I've forgotten. Alfi was supposed to pick her up."

"Pick her up where?"

"From the airport."

Justin took out his notepad, feeling like he was gaining headway. He made a note to cross-check with his Malay colleagues when the Hajj had taken place.

"Where is Alfi, Mr Roslan?"

"My boy, my only boy, Alfi." He nodded, taking a sip of hot tea. "He's here with me," and he pointed to his chest. Roslan got up from his seat to tend to his chirping bird. "This one sells for $800 on the market, you know?" He smiled, proudly presenting the *mata puteh* to Justin. "It needs a shower now, don't you, my *sayang*?"

Justin saw this as his cue to leave and look for Alfi in the tiny three-room flat if indeed he was at home. He went into the room on his right without asking Roslan's permission, assuming that it belonged to Alfi.

One of the house cats sat on the bed watching Justin. At the corner was an empty fish tank and a TV set, flanked by rifle championship medals hung above it. Justin stared at the photograph on the wall next to the medals. In the picture, Alfi, handsome like his father, posed with his championship medals, surrounded by his teammates at the Singapore Gun Club.

Suddenly, the keys to the front door jangled and Justin looked out of the bedroom to see that Alfi was home.

The young man greeted his father the Muslim way, by putting

both his palms out to lightly graze his father's palms. "Is someone here, Abah?" Justin heard him say from the hallway.

"It's that Chinese *mata* again," Roslan said.

Justin walked into the living room and held up his identification badge. "Alfi Roslan, I'm Corporal Justin Kong from the Singapore Police Force," he announced.

The young man walked past him and tried to slam the door of his room, but Justin blocked the opening with his palms. "Alfi Roslan, I am here to ask you a few questions."

"Please do not disturb us anymore, Corporal."

"We received a missing person's report last week."

"Let me guess, was it a Mister Ibrahim who filed the report?"

"I cannot disclose that information."

"Then I cannot help you, Corporal."

"Your father said you were supposed to pick her up from the airport last week."

"My father is an old man. I wouldn't believe everything he says."

"Alfi Roslan, your cooperation is much appreciated in this case. Aren't you at all concerned about your mother?"

"Corporal, I love my mother. But there are a lot of crazies in Marsiling. People with nothing better to do. Bored and out of their minds." He made a circle with his finger and let out a whistle.

"Alfi Roslan!" Justin shouted, but Alfi pushed his bedroom door closed.

* * *

Justin drove back to his office on Jalan Bahar and powered up his computer. The Jurong Police Division HQ was quiet as usual, with most of the officers out patrolling the streets.

It was on days like these when he really needed to see Delia. Snowskin Delia who took away all his stress of working in the force and who provided him much comfort. He felt powerless to solve the case and bitter about having to take it on. Why was a missing person's case not handed over to the Investigations Department in Cantonment? He was only a Corporal, and Marsiling wasn't even his jurisdiction. Tonight he would go to see Delia.

For now, he had his cup of coffee with him, along with two piping hot potato curry puffs from his favourite store on Jurong West Avenue 5. Justin took out his notepad and was about to type Rubianah Bakar's name into the system directory when a booming voice gave him a fright.

"Ah, the Ruby case!" It was Sergeant Wong standing behind him, watching his screen.

"Sir, I didn't see you at all." Justin wiped up the spilled coffee on his desk.

"That's alright, Kong," he smiled. "I'm always full of surprises."

"Is that what you call it, the Ruby case?"

"It's very sad, yes. Her case is well-known in the force. She has been missing for quite a while now."

"But it was reported only a week ago."

"There will always be fresh reports." He touched his stubble, smiling at Justin. Sergeant Wong had a fatherly voice, and he looked at Justin with kind eyes. This was the man who took charge of him when he was first transferred over from the

Tactical Unit in Queensway. Justin had been suspended after he had left his colleague, Imran, with a broken rib after a brawl at the station car park. Soon after, Justin was transferred to Jurong, a less strenuous unit.

"We have to keep searching, boy. Don't give up. Perseverance – that's the spirit behind the Singapore Police Force." Sergeant Wong looked at Justin as a father would a son.

* * *

The sun had set on Day Five and the blue of dusk was over the horizon of the multi-storey flats. The ashes of Justin's cigarette had gone cold underneath his shoe, as he continued to camp out on Marsiling Hill. This time, he found a park bench by the corner, which did not provide as good a view but still enabled him to look straight into the flat. Suddenly, a figure stirred from the living room window and Justin quickly picked up his binoculars.

It was the old man's son, Alfi. He seemed to be in a hurry and minutes later he went out of the flat. Justin walked quickly down the pebble steps of Marsiling Hill, which was decorated in the style of a circular garden path, tailing Alfi from the void deck to the multi-storey carpark opposite their block. From behind a pillar, he saw Alfi throw a black trash bag into the boot of a car before driving out onto the main road.

Justin got into his own vehicle and pursued from two or three cars away. It had started to drizzle and he almost lost him a few times along the Bukit Timah and Kranji Expressways, but kept a close eye on the back of Alfi's black Nissan. For twenty minutes they drove like an invisible convoy, before Alfi turned off the highway into the Lim Chu Kang area.

Keeping his distance, Justin saw Alfi stop his car by the main gate of Pusara Abadi, the Muslim cemetery ground. Justin swerved to the side and waited until he saw Alfi getting out of the car empty-handed. Justin crept up behind Alfi's car and pried the boot open with an Allen key that he always carried in his pocket. Inside was a black trash bag and a long machete, well-worn and used, crusted along its edges with a dark stain. It was soil, not blood, as he lifted his finger to taste it.

Justin put the machete back, closed the boot and went closer into the burial grounds, the long weeds brushing the sides of his trousers. Alfi stood at the edge of the cemetery. Justin stopped, crouched behind a large tombstone and watched. A darker, smaller man appeared next to Alfi. They talked for a few minutes; several crumpled dollar notes were exchanged. Alfi patted the man's back. The man departed. Then Alfi walked back to his car.

Justin continued to watch. Alfi returned with the machete. Taking his time, he hacked away at the overgrown scrub around a blue minaret tombstone. Slow and lethargic like a landscape gardener, he pulled up the weeds and threw them into a pile at the side. Justin waited until Alfi cleared the vegetation and left the grounds, before inching forward. On the minaret tombstone, he saw the engraved name, "Rubianah binte Bakar" – she had died eight years ago.

* * *

Back at the Jurong Police Division HQ, Justin knocked impatiently on the door of Sergeant Wong's office. When there was no answer, he barged in, only to see his superior sipping a cup of coffee over a newspaper, his legs crossed.

"Sergeant, I need to talk to you about the Ruby case."

Sergeant Wong wiped the coffee foam from his moustache. "Good morning, Corporal," he said with a smile.

"Rubianah Bakar. I found her tombstone."

"Where?"

"At the Pusara Abadi."

"The where?"

"The Muslim cemetery. In Lim Chu Kang."

"But how could that be?" he quizzed.

"I followed their son, Alfi, and tailed him to the cemetery."

"You've been working hard, Corporal." He clapped, almost too loudly. "That's brilliant development."

"What do you mean development? There is no development. The case is closed."

"Well, have you checked the records?"

"Not yet, but I will."

"Well then, I wouldn't be so quick to make a conclusion."

"But ..."

Sergeant Wong waved him away. "No buts, Corporal Kong. As long as there are still fresh enquiries we must keep investigating."

"But there is nothing more to investigate. Isn't a tombstone concrete enough evidence?"

"We don't know if this is the same Rubianah Bakar. Who knows, it might be another woman with the same name!" Sergeant Wong clapped his hands and laughed, getting up from his chair.

Justin felt his anger rise. "You're wasting my time, Sergeant."

"Your time? But what else is there for you to do, Corporal?

Pay another visit to the prostitute?"

Justin went red in the face.

"We like to keep our force occupied with the right things," Sergeant Wong continued. "And since your disciplinary record at Queensway, there's not been much that a blacklisted officer can be trusted with, is there?"

"So you led me on a wild goose chase to keep me occupied?"

"Looks like it's working. Now get back to work, Corporal. The Ruby case is not closed as long as I say it isn't."

* * *

At Marsiling Hill, Justin waited until Alfi left his flat before following him rapidly down the steps of the hillock and onto the void deck. Pursuing him to the multi-storey car park with a pair of handcuffs in his back pocket, Justin crept up behind the young man and pushed him against a concrete beam.

Alfi's baseball cap fell off. Startled by the sudden attack, he struggled to fight back but could not turn around. Justin leaned his full weight on Alfi as he cuffed the young man's hands behind his back.

"Wasting police time is an offence, Alfi Roslan!" Justin spoke through gritted teeth. The memories of fighting Imran came back to him, except this time he would break more than just a rib.

"Why did you make that call? Why did you make a false report, Alfi?"

"There are things a son must do for his father," Alfi said. "If he loves and honours him. Now what would you know about that?"

Justin spat on the ground. How dare this man make such insinuations about his relationship with his father? If not for Sergeant Wong's confiscation on his first day at Jurong, he would have pulled out his gun and put it against Alfi's head.

"I'm going to call you in," Justin sneered.

"I wouldn't do that to him. Would you?"

Justin turned Alfi around and grabbed him by the collar now, his anger flushing.

"You have no idea what I have to put up with," Alfi said. "You don't know how hard it is to keep my father sane. Only the hope of my mother alive is able to keep him going."

Justin punched the beam by the side of Alfi's head. Alfi did not wince, but only laughed, his glazed eyes lighting up. For a moment he looked like his father, Roslan, admiring his captive birds at the balcony.

"Corporal, there are a lot of crazies in Marsiling," Alfi said, letting out a whistle.

About the Author

Wan Phing Lim was born to Malaysian parents in 1986 in Butterworth, Penang. She is a full-time writer living in Singapore, where her poems and short stories have been published by Ethos Books, Math Paper Press and the National Library Board. She was also a finalist at the Esquire x Montblanc Fiction Project for her story, "Oil & Water".

SPACE, TIME AND CHICKEN RICE

KANE WHEATLEY-HOLDER

I first met Christina at Tan Tock Seng Hospital on September 12th 2015, the same day my father died of heart failure after a long, drawn-out ordeal. His last words were, "Tomorrow I'll …" before his eyes closed like a rusty gate, and he wheezed his final breath. My family stayed in my father's ward, in silence, contemplating his torn-off words. After the moment had passed, I roamed around and found a lobby far away. I sat among a row of stiff plastic seats and sipped a can of Milo.

She sat opposite me, between an old Chinese lady with an eye patch and a Malay man with a cast on his arm. She scarfed down spoonfuls of chicken rice from a takeaway tub.

"I recommend the chicken rice in the canteen," she said after a while. I looked up. A sticky grain of rice clung to her lower lip like a derelict ship. "I don't usually like hospital food, but this is good. I can't put my finger on why, though."

I refused to cry. This area was too public. I would wait until I went home and was in bed. Our eyes met.

She was sixteen – a year older than me – with short-cropped hair, a round pale face and lips that barely existed. She was tall and gangly, like me. She wore a dress with a duplicating pink orchid on it. Of course, I didn't know it then. It was just a flower.

"Maybe it's the chili," I replied after eight seconds.

"Cannot be. I think it's the rice. Maybe they steam it in a special way. The chicken meat is tender and moist, too. Damn nice."

"I wouldn't know. I don't cook."

"I try to. When I can," she said and finally looked at me.

"What are you here for?" I panic-asked.

"My mother's diabetic. She fell down the stairs. She doesn't eat right. She's okay, lah."

I remember numerous topics came up after that. We talked some more about what she was studying in polytechnic, why she loved chicken rice, and her fascination with flowers. Her favourites were Vanda Miss Joaquim (Singapore's national flower), Paphiopedilum Kobold's Doll (an orchid that looked like it had a bulbous pink tongue), and Ascofinetia Cherry Blossom.

I asked her why the fascination with flowers. She stopped, as if she had forgotten what she had rehearsed. "I just think we could appreciate a flower a little more."

* * *

We started to go out a few months later. I don't know why we stayed friends for so long. I'm not good on the whole at small talk. My friends called me a "stiff".

Christina and I didn't do traditional datey things. There were no fancy dinners or theme parks, nor were there any grand displays of affections with roses and written cards. Instead, we went to the Botanic Gardens and Gardens by the Bay. A lot.

"I've already signed on to the Air Force, so after I finish my Aerospace degree, I'm going to see where it takes me."

"Sounds like you," she smiled. "Aiyoh, planes are all you talk about."

We were watching a park performance of Roald Dahl's *James and the Giant Peach* on the grass, along with about fifty other people. The air was thick and stuffy, but neither of us complained.

"I think I'm headed into medicine," she said. "I've always wanted to find a cure for diabetes."

"That's great. Researchers might be able to do it from what I've read," I said. "They've just discovered a hidden biological process within our cells that aids the healing process. If scientists can isolate and tap into it somehow, people could heal from injuries and diseases much faster. Super cool."

"Jonathan Lim, that's the sexiest thing anyone has ever said to me. *Bo liao*, but sexy."

She laughed and turned back to James. I watched her for a few more moments. My smile lagged behind the rest of my thoughts. That's me in a nutshell really: I lag.

On stage, a giant peach levitated across tall metallic blocks that simulated New York City. We watched it for a while, remarking on the fact that we couldn't see any strings.

"Come to my place tomorrow," she said without looking at me. "I want to make you my chicken rice. I've nearly perfected the recipe."

"Ah, the mystery continues," I chuffed.

"I know right! I've been everywhere – Marina Square, Katong, Jurong, Clementi, Orchard, hospitals – and eaten plates of it. I still can't get the taste just right. Tomorrow for lunch, okay?"

"Tomorrow it is then."

We watched the rest of the performance then took the MRT back to her place. I forgot to hold her hand. As I said, I lag.

The next day, I visited Christina. She had the meal ready in the kitchen. I sat down, took a spoonful of rice, with a little soy sauce mixed with chili, and topped it off with a thin chicken breast slice. I can't say I am a foody type of person. I appreciate the culinary simplicity of a $2.20 *nasi lemak* in my local hawker centre. This was different. The chicken was tender, with a hint of salt that accentuated the slightly raw meat inside. The rice was fluffy and light. It was like nothing I had ever tasted.

"Wah, *shiok*! You could sell it."

"You think so," Christina said, biting her lip, her body teetering on the balls of her feet. "I didn't overdo the rice? I steamed it overnight in some herbs and a dash of coconut milk."

"No, no, it's very good!"

She cupped my face in between her hands and kissed me. I was still chewing. A tidal wave of blood flushed through my brain, tickling the space between my eyes. I kissed her back.

Damn the lag.

* * *

It must have been four years into our relationship when I was doing my second year of National Service and training as an Air Force pilot. The pay was good, and we did anything we wanted during my days-off. Most of the time, we enjoyed lazing around in my bed and watching old movies. She loved Disney musicals.

I loved sci-fi dramas about our dark, bleak, foreboding future. It was the perfect mix.

One night, I was stuck in camp and had to book out at midnight. She messaged.

> Ok, go home and rest. I'll c u tomorrow
> *Christina - Message sent at 12:34 AM*
>
> Sure. I'm sorry. My Encik talk for so long sia. Can still meet you :)
> *Jonathan - Message sent at 12:36 AM*
>
> No. It's ok.
> *Christina - Message sent at 12:50 AM*

A full stop? I knew there was always something wrong with a full stop. I should have called her then. She called me whilst I was waiting for the traffic light, five minutes from home.

"I need you," she said. Her words were cracked, barely audible, hardly there at all.

"Are you okay? You're crying."

"Please come. Now." Her breathing came in big, rasping gulps.

"Don't worry. I'll be there right away."

She hung up. I flagged the next taxi and rushed to her flat. When I got there, I found the front door unlocked. She sat on the couch in her living room, legs curled up to her chest, staring into nothing.

"I'm terrible," she said, each word punctuated with a heavy wheeze. Her eyes were lost in shadow. Her beige skirt was covered in blotches of damp tears. I sat down and brushed sweat-soaked hair away from her face.

"No, no, you're not," I said.

"I get scared. I can't breathe. I can't control it."

"I know," I said.

It was the first time I had really seen it. Christina was the most ebullient person I knew, but her anxiety attacks were always sudden, a silent terror waiting to seize control. It was through her I learnt the warmest smiles often hide the darkest of echoes.

"I'm a terrible girlfriend."

"No, you are not."

Christina's breathing gradually calmed. Her eyes settled on a dark corner in the living room, and she focused on it, completely, until she was ready. After she seemed better, I helped her up.

We talked only after she showered. I didn't resent her for her attacks. She felt too much. I felt guilty for not feeling the same way.

As I lay with her, stretched out on a mattress near her bed, I thought about how I had no real friends or family members that I was close to. I really was a stiff, someone who would never be dashing, or exciting, or funny, or brave, or dangerous, or anything other than a stiff. I remember thinking, just before the dance of sleep took me away, that people should listen to the voices in their heads more often.

* * *

Christina and I married when I was twenty-five and she was twenty-six. The wedding was humble but dazzling in my memory, infused with all the soft orchids Christina had wanted. Soon after, I began training to pilot the FX-601 Grey Fox, a new military helicopter. Christina was promoted to a supervising nurse position in NUH. We got a flat a year later, as I was studying for my Masters. In all those years, there was something that never faltered: Christina's love for chicken rice.

Over time I realised the act of me eating seemed to heal her anxiety. Whatever we were going through, whatever grated at our minds, the food pushed it all away. Her attacks ceased. We didn't need to go out to fancy restaurants or bars. We were enough. We only went out to visit orchid exhibitions at Gardens by the Bay, or the newest flower arrangements at Botanic Gardens. She lit up whenever she saw a new, colourful species.

Every night, as she lay in my arms, the sheets washed with an inky stillness, I prayed. I was not a religious man, but it just felt right. I thought about my father and what he would have thought of Christina. I thought about my mother, reunited with him now, and wondered if she was sad for never having grandchildren.

And at the end of those thoughts and prayers, I dreamt of Singapore, of blocks of flats consumed by glorious epiphytes, plants that joined every household in thin veins of green.

* * *

I was called into General Ishmail's office a few years after I received my Major rank. I had already been through several humanitarian tours in East Timor, Afghanistan and operations across ASEAN regions. General Ishmail greeted me at the door with a glinting smile.

"Take a seat. It's good to see you. *Teh*?"

"Yes, sir."

I watched the General. His chunky fingers looked dainty as he mixed condensed milk into a cup of tea. He finished making the *teh* and gave it to me, his leather chair squeaking with his every move. His eyes focused on a thick black folder in front of him. He sipped his coffee mug printed with the words "National Day Parade 2020".

"Let me get straight to it. As we already know, there's been a lot of talk about security in the region. I don't need to tell you the specifics. We're a small nation that needs to look ahead. We need to source out problems before they creep up and bite us on the backside," he smiled.

He stopped. I nodded, smiled.

"Natural resources used to be our perennial problem. Not anymore. There are new enemies rearing their ugly heads every month. If it isn't the Middle East, it's in Europe. If it's not there, there's the instability of South East Asia."

I sipped my tea and nodded. This wasn't my first operation with a catered introduction. My experience with a variety of fighter planes and piloted drones was invaluable in sustaining order in conflicted regions.

"We have a special operation for you. An operation that will ensure stability for a very long time," he said. "We just need a pilot."

"A pilot, sir?" I smiled. "A pilot for what?"

"Well, it's not really a pilot at all. Wrong word," General Ishmail said and laughed. "An astronaut. We need an astronaut."

* * *

I was sworn to secrecy. For a year, I underwent a multitude of physical and mental tests to ascertain my ability to pilot the experimental shuttle. I studied astronautics, orbital mechanics, aerospace engineering, as well as underwater training. My mission was simple: assemble a power system capable of sustaining a satellite link in space. The system – referred to as LION1 – was a power conversion system made from an electrically heated free-flow mercury boiler. I was in charge of it. So far, the system's simulated performance in 1 g, 2 g, and zero g was holding up. Space was another matter.

Only to Christina did I tell everything. She listened every day, like I was telling a riveting bedtime story. The night before the shuttle launch, she asked, "Will you be safe? It's space. Isn't it all cold and dark and no one can hear you scream? I remember that from a film."

"I'll be safe. I'll see you as soon as I come back. In five days."

"I'll make you something. Something to put in your astronauto-super-star-trek-ship fridge."

"All right," I said.

Then Christina and I made love on the couch. As she slept, I traced my fingers across her arms, through her long hair, in the grooves and shadows that told me she was alive. I listened to her sleep until the sun rose.

It was Monday November 11th, 2032. I got ready in silence. I was stiff. She made me *nasi lemak* for breakfast. We kissed. Longer. I prepared to leave. At the front gate, I turned to say goodbye. I held her for a few moments. When I pulled away, she smiled, bright and full, reminding me of the statistical perfection of an empty Milo can. Then we kissed again until her smell of syrup clung to my lips.

I drove to the base situated in the deserted heart of a military training ground in Lim Chu Kang. Far into the jungle, it was the perfect spot for a loud and potentially eye-catching launch. The odd taxi driver or passer-by would assume it was an uproarious military exercise. Assumptions were good.

When I arrived, I met with three Generals, five unnamed individuals in suits, three Russians, and my co-pilot, Ralph. An American astronaut, Ralph had a family with five children.

We got changed into our suits in silence. My suit was form-fitting and metallic, meshed together at the shoulder blades with various heat resistant plates. Every breath, heartbeat and brain wave pattern was recorded through that suit. For some reason, it gave me little reassurance.

We walked through the base's hangar until we reached the miniaturised shuttle. Around me, a thousand different sounds melded into a steady din. I looked up and saw a rectangular window with a shaded plane of glass. I knew who was watching.

I took my seat inside and waited with the five other astronauts. As commands were barked into my ears, Christina's face appeared in my mind.

"What are you smiling about?" Ralph asked, as we secured ourselves in and began the launch procedures. The ship's computer consoles lit up like a swarm of metallic fireflies.

"Space, time and chicken rice," I said.

They all laughed, the first time they had done that with me.

The shuttle launched as planned. When the charging roar of the shuttle calmed, we drifted up and past the upper atmosphere into space. I looked outside the ship.

The sun's rays scattered across the atmosphere, endless and powerful, like a thousand tiny prisms bathed in gold. The clouds were pure and stainless, content in their space.

Thrum ...

The shuttle's engines ceased. They powered up again. Weaker. A high-pitched rumble drained into a sonorous drone.

I remembered the training; something was wrong. The engines were fighting against the gravitational forces that enmeshed the shuttle. The engine cried again. A piercing shockwave sliced through my senses, my brain, the tissue under my tongue.

My ears popped. My head jerked. My helmet rammed into the ship's headrest.

Thrum, Thrum, Thrum.

A cold liquid trickled down my ear and across the back of my neck.

"Mission control, do you copy? Something has hit ..."

The shuttle walls wheezed like a tar-filled lung. The ship's warning systems blared, consoles sparked, glass shattered. I turned to the computer's schematics, but found only a panel of buttons immersed in flames. I lifted the visor of my helmet just as three globules of blood, a perfect triangle, drifted past my eyes.

Ralph screamed. The others shouted for help, adjusted their communication equipment, mumbled to their Gods. I turned to the vacuum-sealed glass window.

Outside a pastiche of shimmering colours, strands of celestial web caught hold of the ship. The crackling of the ship was consumed by a shriek between my eyes. And then, quite simply, the darkness seized me without a fight.

* * *

Thrum. Thrum.

I remember seeing my father, standing by his wheelchair, tapping a rolled-up newspaper in his hand.

* * *

Thrum.

I remember seeing a Vanda Miss Joaquim, its rosy-violet petals, its fiery orange centre, and, resting on its spotted lip, the Universe in a droplet of water.

* * *

I woke up to shimmering white faces. My vision slowly got better. A team of blurry doctors saw to my every whim. I didn't ask any questions. They all seemed Singaporean: an Indian surgeon, a Chinese doctor, and a Eurasian neurologist. My recovery was paramount. It took weeks for my injuries to heal. I didn't know that at the time.

After two months and five days, I was up and about. No shock, no twinges of pain from fractured bones, no streaks of discomfort from ruptured organs. But I could walk. That was an unequivocal something.

"He'll see you now," said a secretary.

I walked into an oval-shaped room. It was large and comfortable, with frames of awards, military hardware, and pictures from magazines adorning the stark black walls. A huge mahogany desk stood before me, and in a chair, a man in a uniform I did not recognise.

A badge on his right sleeve said: SINGAPORE. His wrinkled forehead looked like a topographical map leading to two hooked commas for eyebrows.

"Major Lim. Jonathan. How incredible to see you," he boomed. "I'm Admiral Theodore Liang. Singapore Air Force."

"Your uniform is different," I said.

"Yes, yes, it is. We changed it."

"When?"

"Would you like something to drink?"

He turned to a small table beside him. On it was a machine I did not recognise. There were paper cups. *Teh.* I wanted some *Teh.* I watched his fingers jitter on the edge of his seat, tracing the lines of the stitching. The leather squeaked.

"We wanted to debrief you sooner, but your health was important to us. We needed to know that your body could take it. You've made an amazing recovery." I nodded. The Admiral nodded. He took a moment to compose himself. "Your shuttle reached the upper atmosphere as planned. Your objective was to assemble a power system for a communication link we could use for military surveillance. But something happened."

"Where are they? Raphael Long, John Tiam, Veronika Edita Zakharovna, Sobakov David Svyatoslavovich ..."

"Yes," he waited a while. "I'm sorry. They didn't survive."

"What happened?"

"We monitored you from the mission control and had you up there for a full eleven minutes. Then your shuttle disappeared from our Laser-Guided Cameras."

"Where did you find me?"

"In the South China Sea. You were unconscious, pushed into an escape pod. It was Ralph. He died from his burns on re-entry. Jonathan, I don't know how to say this ..."

"Stop calling me 'Jonathan'."

"Major Lim," he cupped his head in his hands and breathed. He looked at the file on his desk, turned back to me, as if it was futile to read from it. "The year is 2136. One hundred and four years have passed."

His calm façade crumbled. His voice trembled into an incoherent void. "We don't know."

* * *

Singapore was no longer the home I knew. The roads were now thin stainless steel tracks. Buildings were reinforced chasms of glass. The whole island was encased in an unsullied bubble. The sky was pale bronze, as if viewed through a rheumy patina.

I requested to take a driverless car – all the rage now, apparently – out of the Air Force base and into the heart of Woodlands. It was denied. They wanted me followed. A young man in a dark suit introduced himself as Nigel. He was tasked to bring me somewhere else. We got into the car, a sleek three-wheeled machine with tracks. As the car drove itself, a nebulous blue map of our location shimmered on the windshield. Nigel performed a ballet of looking at his electronic tablet and fastidiously adjusting his suit.

We passed sights I barely recognised: tall blocks, with roofs that resembled reinforced domes; various gated mosques;

pyramid-shaped churches; and a MRT track that was hardly there at all. I saw crowds of people along the streets, some talking, some reading electronic tablets, some dressed in outfits that looked similar to what I used to wear.

We stopped at a car park fifteen minutes later. A girder displayed a sign above us.

Lim Chu Kang Graveyard for the Rested

"Come," Nigel said and got out. I followed him.

Christina's burial site was a steel pod buried partially underground. On the dried, dusty soil were small electronic cones that flashed orange every minute, like the intricate spine of an insect. There was no need for stones or coffins or urns anymore. Everything was photonic. Even in death.

Nigel told me to press the button on the cone when I was ready. He trod back the way he came and waited for me at the entrance.

I pressed the button.

She appeared before me in a veil of light, quivering, as if the machine hadn't fully warmed up yet. Her face bloomed in sketchy strands, before converging into a sharper image. The background was an open field at the Botanic Gardens, where we had watched *James and the Giant Peach*. I had taken the picture. She had worn a dress with daffodils and buttercups then. She wore it now.

A spinning plate of light appeared below her face:

Christina Lim
Date of Birth: September 4th 1999

Departed: March 3rd 2035
Biography: None
Next of Kin: None
Last Words: None

The image continued to flicker. A few pixels were damaged. Five black blocks bored into her right shoulder.

My mind churned, a voiceless storm. My body shook. My stomach clenched. I turned away, vomiting as far away from her as I could. When I got back to the car, Nigel's face was a mask of stone. He said nothing. I turned around and saw Christina fade into the sallow light.

We drove.

* * *

Minutes later, we arrived at a restaurant called GERALDS. A glowing neon sign at the front displayed a grinning Chinese man eating a plate of noodles. Nigel said we were in Clementi, an estate area that was rarely visited anymore.

"Why are we here?" I asked.

Nigel didn't answer. We went inside and sat down at a large round table with an electronic screen integrated inside. It flashed a Tiger Beer ad. Nigel positioned his tablet and took a picture of me. A few waiters, staff members in pristine white waistcoats, cleaned tables nearby.

"I think it was in the year 2034, early January," Nigel began, reading off the tablet. "New discoveries opened doors in the areas of medicine, neurology, transport, eco-friendly fuels, and electronics. The food and beverage business was understandably next. As viral diseases like Zika, avian flu and severe bouts of famine struck Asian countries across the world, a Singaporean entrepreneur called Mrs Carey Ong developed a new form of clean water technology. She also had an invested interested in food research."

Nigel waited for a few minutes. A waiter eventually came back with a tray.

"She soon got backing for a patented technology known as Freezol. Essentially, it was a chemical agent with the ability to flash freeze organic matter at a molecular level. Suspended animation, if you will. Freezol eradicated the development of mould and the need to refrigerate food. And thus, Singapore was granted the unique ability to store food indefinitely, while other countries suffered."

The waiter served Nigel a plate of *nasi lemak* with *ikan bilis*.

For me, the waiter lowered several items: a plate of chicken rice, along with a small container of soy sauce and chili. I peered into the rice. Steam twisted and unfurled, as if I was watching a spirit made of silk. The smell washed my senses clean. For the first time in weeks, my stomach ached.

"Over the next couple of years, people used Freezol to archive food. Some employed large companies to do it for them, you know, just in case we were ravaged by an unexpected war. The rich used it, mostly. The war never happened. Today only a handful of old restaurants, like this one, use the forgotten stock to create a more authentic culinary experience," he stopped, pointing to his food. "Your wife arranged this with our help."

Nigel turned to the waiter and smiled. "One *kopi siew dai*.

Jonathan?"

It took me a while. "*Teh peng.*"

"Very good, sir."

The waiter left. I turned back to my chicken rice. The fork felt like granite in my hand.

"*Makan,*" Nigel said, nodding towards my plate. He began eating.

I lowered the fork and took a lump of rice and chicken. I dabbed it in the soy sauce, allowing some of the chili to trickle down over the side. Steam still rose from it, thick and full and strong. I tasted it. The rice, the meat, the sauce – I had tasted them all before, some time, some place, when they used to mean something.

Then I didn't eat; I savoured the chicken rice. The delicate trembling of my fingers stopped. Swallowed. Again. My soul was torn apart and reborn in chicken rice with a hint of coconut.

When I was done, I thanked the waiter and Nigel. We got up to leave and made our way back to the car.

There were many questions Nigel wanted to ask me. What would I do now? How would I adjust? Would I even do anything at all?

I told him I wanted to go to the Gardens by the Bay. That is, if it was still there.

"Indeed it is, along with the Botanic Gardens. We would never get rid of both places. May I ask why?" Nigel said.

"I'd like to see some flowers," I replied.

"Flowers?" Nigel said quizzically, and turned back to his tablet with a crooked smile. "I don't see a problem with that."

As the car drove itself, I looked out of the window, at buildings that pierced the sky like iron spears, at passing cars that made no sound, at a sky that held no clouds, and thought, without any doubt, that I would stay with the orchids for the rest of the day. I had time.

About the Author

Kane Wheatley-Holder has enjoyed a career as a media producer and television scriptwriter. In 2015, he completed the Mentor Access Project, a twelve-month writing programme organised by the National Arts Council. His short stories have been published in the *Quarterly Literary Review Singapore*, short story anthology *Roti Bakar/Pulp Toast* and *50 Metres: Our Swimming Pools*. One of his short stories was highly commended in *The Epigram Books Collection of Best New Singaporean Short Stories: Volume 2*. He is currently seeking literary representation for his debut YA sci-fi novel and is working on a collection of short stories about parallel worlds in Singapore.

A different version of "Space, Time and Chicken Rice" was previously published in *Quarterly Literary Review Singapore*, Vol. 13, No. 4, Oct 2014.

TOO FAT

VANESSA DEZA HANGAD

Eunice Baker-Lim instinctively covered her lunchbox when she saw the office waifs in ridiculously high heels and short pastel dresses. She had no need to do so because it contained grilled salmon over a kale salad. Nothing to be ashamed of. Eunice kept a careful accounting of her food intake and avoided the junk those girls ate at the *kopitiam* on the first floor of their building. If she died right then and there, she, the virtuous clean-eater (minus one minor treat of super-sized fries she conveniently forgot to record), could not be judged and found lacking. The pearly gates would open for her. It would be purgatory at best for those girls. And not only for their downright meanness but for their inappropriate office outfits. Upper-thigh grazing dresses with cut-outs on the side that displayed flashes of bare skin. Perhaps they shopped in the same stores as those other type of working girls gyrating on stage at Orchard Towers (which always sounded to Eunice like a respectable place of business or an expensive condominium). Then there was the local food they subsisted on. Greasy noodles. Deep fried everything. And yet they never had to suck in their gut or cover it with a purse the way Eunice did when riding the bus. Those Account Reps whose professional aspirations included snagging an expat husband in Clarke Quay barely made it to the gym except to stare at themselves in the mirror at yoga class and yet, because life was unfair to girls like Eunice, managed to keep their figures trim.

She was certain they looked down on her. At her flat, lifeless hair and swollen feet stuffed into low-heeled Mary Janes instead of gracefully angling forty-five degrees into street-walking stilettos. Half-Singaporean, half-American Eunice who was twice their size. Constantly hot and sweaty Eunice, unaccustomed to the weather even after having lived in Singapore for almost a year. An abject failure at attracting a man and keeping mascara from running down her face. The head Mean Girl made a gesture, flicking at the inner corner of her eye, like eww, fix your make up. The rest giggled as they walked past, streams of caramel and bottle blonde hair swishing behind their backs.

Eunice couldn't go to lunch with them even if they were nice enough to ask her. Part of her job was to answer phones during the lunch hour. By 1:30 PM when she could take a break, everyone else had gone back to work. So every day, she ate her lunch at the front desk then sat by herself in a near empty McDonald's, eating cone after cone of soft serve ice cream until she felt sick. This was another omission from her food diary.

She had applied for an Account Rep job but was told she was overly-qualified. She suspected that the real reason was because she didn't fit the profile, wasn't pretty enough to be given a "customer-facing" role at Ships Ahoy Limited. Unable to handle any more rejection, Eunice begged for anything available. And so she became a Project Assistant, which in her company meant a dotted line to every single manager, a peon to be called upon for anything and everything. From answering phones and eating lunch at the front desk so that the model/receptionist could go on a proper break, to writing financial reports and buying gifts for baby showers, she was the dismally paid Jill of all Trades.

She thought back to the day she decided to apply for a job at the cargo freight shipping company, filling out the application form at home while their maid, Joselita, chopped Napa cabbage for a Chinese Chicken salad.

"This could cause a lawsuit in the US! Look, it asks for it right here. Are you married and do you have children?"

Joselita muttered a distracted, "Uhuh. Okay, Ms Eunice."

"Then after father's occupation, they want to know your O-Level scores. Okay, that's fine, I guess. Oh, but here's the best part."

"Heh?" Joselita peeked out from the refrigerator door. She took chicken breast out of a Ziploc bag to shred.

Eunice felt like throwing the application form away. "They seriously want me to attach a picture and put down how much I weigh? What the hell? So if you're too fat, they won't even bother calling you in for an interview?"

She quit eating carbs for a month and submitted a photoshopped picture that made her face look slimmer. Once she came in for the official interview, the game was up. Passed over for the position she applied for and given a low-paying grunt job, she found no reason to keep avoiding French fries. She gained all the weight back and then some.

* * *

An elegant flower shop in Robertson Quay. If someone were to ask Eunice about her favourite spot in Singapore, this would be it. The smells reminded her of California, the place where she had lived most of her life until her father's illness forced her to return to Singapore. A year at the most, her mother had promised. Yet she and Eunice's older sister Priscilla, the attorney who married another attorney and spawned two perfect snowflakes, remained happily in Berkeley. *Sorry, but I can't take time off from work. I'm on the partner track now. Sorry, I have to take care of Lisette and Giselle. Your sister is stressed out with work. She's gonna make partner soon, did she tell you? It's not so bad in Singapore. Just hang in there for a while longer. And we have to forgive Papa at some point, don't we?*

Eunice couldn't say no to her mother, for whom love was strategic. She withheld just enough so that Eunice always hungered for the approval that her sister consumed with nonchalance.

Unmarried and a recent college grad, Eunice was volunteered to care for her father after he received the diagnosis – Alzheimer's. That womanizer and rageaholic couldn't even remember why they left him in Singapore in the first place. Thirteen years had gone by since Eunice last saw her father. She was ten years old when her American mom yanked them out of the prestigious Raffles Girls Primary to start over in California. Into a crunchy granola life of vegan potlucks and Sunday book clubs. Her mother reinvented herself as a New Age healer who escaped the artifice of Singapore for the earthiness of Berkeley. She became a hit with the faculty wives, and as her reputation spread, she launched a successful business selling organic spice mixes for Singaporean hawker foods she overhauled for the ethically vegetarian clientele. Eunice came of age in a Victorian house that looked like a wedding cake, with French lavender and yellow tuberoses growing behind the white picket fence.

When she heard the unmistakable nasal voice of Brenda the Project Manager, Eunice closed her eyes and transported herself to the misty coolness and the fragrance of her mother's garden. The former stay-at-home mom was a recent hire. Eager to prove to everyone that she could do more than organise play dates and bring cupcakes to her daughter's pre-school, Brenda stayed late hours as a show of dedication, which was inversely proportional to her actual productivity. Brenda walked down the row of cubicles while on the phone with her maid. Eunice could tell because of the tone she took. Impatient and not even bothering to ingratiate herself like the way she spoke with everyone else in the office. She continued rattling off ingredients as she leaned against the entrance of Eunice's cubicle, holding up one finger as though it were Eunice who wanted something.

Eunice listened to details of what the helper was to purchase at Cold Storage the next day and an unnecessarily harsh reprimand about her failure to iron the shirt that Ryan wanted to wear that morning.

"Goddammit! I don't care if there are other shirts that you've already ironed. Isn't that what we're paying you for?" Brenda rolled her eyes and pointed at the phone, expecting Eunice to commiserate. She played along, dropping her jaw in the universal Oh My God gesture. "Okay, okay. Enough. Enough! He wanted the dark blue striped Banana Republic shirt, not the light blue one. Dark blue. Dark. Blue. Got that? Remember next time." After another merciless minute, Brenda hung up. "Ugh. Good help is so hard to find these days. But what can you do, right?"

Every crevasse and roll of her mummy belly outlined in a wrap-around dress a few sizes too small, Brenda perched on a low file cabinet, undecided about whether to be a girlfriend or slave driver. "Are you keeping up your food diary? I just ate an entire bag of Cheetos. That's not going into mine."

Eunice noticed the tell-tale orange dust on Brenda's fingers and wondered how a woman who seemed to have it all could be such a slob. A car, a condo, a country club membership, a credit card. The requisite four Cs that meant you had made it in Singapore. Make that five Cs. She had a child, a talkative little girl who Eunice babysat on many occasions. Brianna fell in love with Eunice the moment Brenda introduced them. "She looks like me, Mummy! She's even got the same round tum-tum like mine."

But the cherry on top of Brenda's perfect life was a strapping blonde American husband. Ryan, the former surf instructor turned real estate agent, was the type of expat husband most wives worried about. On several Facebook groups, wives at-risk of losing husbands like him contributed to the feeding frenzies that ensued around discussions of infidelity and divorce. "Watch your back, ladies." Or "Is this your husband? Took this picture at Orchard Towers." In Asia, Ryan was a prime catch and acted like he didn't even know it. He grew up in Southern California and seemed to carry endless summers wherever he went. Brenda's family had enough money to fund his business ventures that were yet to provide a return on investment.

The Account Reps hovered around Brenda's door when Ryan dropped by the office. Eunice smirked at the spectacle they made of themselves, knowing she had a special place they would never occupy. She had seen Ryan almost naked. He passed by her with nothing but a towel around his waist one Sunday while he was getting ready for brunch. Their eyes met and Eunice looked away, turning her attention back to applying sparkly blue nail polish on Brianna's fingernails. Ryan, Brianna and the envy of the Account Reps. She had it made and yet Brenda couldn't even manage to wash her hands after bingeing on junk food with her office door closed. Around the same size, XL girls in the land of the XXXS, they formed an uneasy alliance. Brenda still blamed her daughter for wrecking her once perfect figure. Eunice didn't even have pregnancy as an excuse for looking the way she did, matronly at twenty-three years old. At least Brenda had everything else going for her.

Eunice slung her hobo purse over her shoulder. "Haven't missed a day. You know how much I love spreadsheets and tracking stuff." She was about to grab her gym bag from under the desk when the dreaded request came.

"Hey, I need a second pair of eyes on a budget proposal. Oh my God! Please say yes?"

Brenda had a habit of waiting until the last minute. The previous week, Eunice was about to shut down her computer when Brenda breezed in, asking for twenty copies of a ten-page project plan. She was Brenda's secret weapon when it came to certain tasks that were too tedious for the lazy yet charismatic Project Manager. She felt obliged to say yes because Brenda was the closest thing she had to a friend. Eunice accompanied Brenda to spas and nail salons, and on rare occasions was treated to a manicure, something Brenda would never let her forget when she asked for the next favour. She and Ryan were regulars at expensive hotel brunch buffets with free-flow champagne. On the days they couldn't convince their maid to give up her Sunday to care for their daughter, Eunice took the MRT and two buses to their landed property in Bukit Timah to play endless games of princess dress-up with Brianna.

"Okay, so anyway, can you email me the updated document tonight? I just sent it before coming over here. And by the way, I got a spa voucher that's about to expire. Ryan and I are going away for the weekend. Do you want it?" Without waiting for Eunice to reply, she handed her a coupon.

"Ten percent off any service." Eunice grimaced as she remembered that spa, where she took care of Brianna while Brenda got a ninety-minute massage and facial. The minimum cost for anything was $120.

"Again, I'm so sorry for springing this on you last minute. You're a doll." Perfect working mother and wife that she was, Brenda had already left the office behind as soon as she passed Eunice the hot potato. She would get home in time to give Brianna a bath and fix Ryan a cocktail.

Eunice unwrapped her emergency Snickers bar. She chewed as a cow resigned to an eternity of humid afternoons watching cars pass by. Eunice zoned out on the pristine beach and turquoise blue waters of her computer screensaver before getting back to work.

* * *

At 6 AM Eunice laced up her sneakers and went for a run. A month had passed since she saved Brenda, who turned around and took full credit for the budget proposal. Away from the office, Brenda rewarded her by inviting Eunice to Sunday Brunch at the Four Seasons. Eunice had starved herself on the appointed weekend. An early morning workout would make her feel less guilty about the obscene amounts of food and champagne she was prepared to consume later in the day.

She could only run for thirty-second stretches at a time. Stopping in the middle of Alkaff Bridge to catch her breath, Eunice looked up at the fantastical bubbles of colour splashed across the bridge. The dayglow pinks and yellows were an eighties dream. Turning up the volume, she sang along to Bowie, high priest of the church of misfits like her. She imagined him in a unitard with the same design as the bridge. Why couldn't she be the master of self-transformation like him? Eunice started off each week with the best of intentions to eat well and workout. By Wednesday all things fell apart. She swore that the buffet would be her last hurrah before going on a juice fast.

Ryan liked Bowie. But he wasn't allowed to keep his concert shirts. The last time Eunice had gone to babysit for them, Brenda got a bug that made her sweep through their two-storey house in search of offending material. Anything old, ripped or out of style had got go. But just as she easily lost steam at the office and relied on Eunice to save her, it too fell upon Eunice to finish organising Brenda's mountains of things. She stayed late, cataloguing their spices by country of origin. Then she rescued Ryan's shirt from the donation pile.

He was in the living room watching *Labyrinth*. Probably mourning the loss of Bowie. On her way out, she passed him the faded concert t-shirt. She imagined how he would look in it, the contrast of the soft material against his muscular shoulders, what it would be like to run her fingers across the tour dates on his back. And again, there was a moment between them. Blue eyes. She was such a sucker for blue eyes. The colour of his daughter's Queen Elsa nail polish.

Later at the hotel buffet, Brianna swiped through the pictures in Eunice's phone. It turned out to be a working brunch for her, something Brenda failed to mention until she met them at the lobby and Brianna grabbed Eunice's hand, squealing, "Aunty Yuny!" How could she not be happy to see the adorable munchkin with big round cheeks like her, who was supposed to stay at home with the maid so that the adults could have boozy brunch in peace? At least two adults were well on their way. Ryan and Brenda returned with their plates loaded with oysters and sexy petals of charcuterie. A waiter topped off their champagne glasses, leaving the bottle on the table after Brenda talked him into it.

"Cheers, everyone! Eunice, don't toast with water. It's bad luck. Wait." Eunice eyed the bottle of Moet with lust. Brenda motioned for the waiter. "A Diet Coke for her, please."

Eunice half-heartedly said cheers, to the dead-end life she had cobbled together for herself. It wasn't supposed to be like this. She blamed it all on her father. If it weren't for him, she would still be in in San Francisco.

"Go ahead and get some food for yourself, Eunice. I'll watch Brianna." Ryan gave her a look of sympathy, ignoring his wife's incredulous stare.

"Are you sure it's okay? Brenda, I can wait until you're done. I don't mind." Eunice took a big gulp out of her Diet Coke.

"No, it's fine. Go ahead." Brenda smiled like she meant it.

Eunice hit the buffet with the razor-sharp mind of a data

scientist, taking her time to sift through the possibilities. She wasn't going to fill up on the cheap stuff. She passed by the pasta station and a tower of baguettes, feeling victorious in her carb avoidance. She considered the salad station then kept moving along. No. Only the deluxe items would do. Smoked salmon topped with caviar and whispers of dill. Oysters Rockefeller. Peking duck in delicate, low carb crepes. The thought hit her as she weaved Hoisin sauce over golden crispy duck skin. She didn't have to indiscriminately accept everything offered to her. She would live her life like she was at a Four Season's Sunday brunch buffet with free-flow champagne. Picking and choosing only the best.

"Here, let me do that for you." Ryan placed flirty curls of scallions over the sweet sauce and folded up the crepe. One hand holding his glass of champagne and the other the Peking duck, he hovered the sinful morsel over her mouth. "May I?"

Eunice shook her head even as he beamed at her with his winning smile. His teeth were unnaturally white and too perfect.

He shrugged then ate her Peking duck, licking his fingers.

"Brenda can be such a bitch sometimes, am I right? Here. I know you've been wanting this." Ryan looked hurt when Eunice once again refused. He downed his champagne and almost dropped the glass.

"I think you've had enough. Where's Brenda?" Eunice put down her plate and scanned the room.

"She saw some of the girls from the office. Took off with them. Something about a sale on designer bags in River Valley. That's all she really cares about. Stupid shit like that."

Eunice stood close and whispered, "Lower your voice, Ryan. People are starting to stare." For a moment, the smell of his sweat and Axe cologne almost drew her back in. Sensing this, he grabbed her by the waist and growled into her shoulder. "Not sure if you know this about me, but all my girlfriends in college were Asian American. Sometimes I wonder how I ended up with Brenda. She's pretty much the opposite of what used to attract me the most. And what still does."

Eunice, on the verge of letting herself melt into the forbidden, looked down to see sparkly blue nails tugging at her skirt.

"Can you go to the potty with me?" Brianna had been crying.

Eunice pushed Ryan away.

"Where did your Mommy go?" Eunice held Brianna's hand and walked with her past Ryan. She shuddered at the thought of what could have happened if his daughter had not walked up to them at the buffet table.

"Don't know." she sniffled. "Sometimes Mommy acts funny. Her face gets red and she talks about weird stuff."

Eunice saw herself at six years old, staying up to wait for her own mother who had promised to tuck her in. At 4 AM, she had stumbled into her daughter's room, full of apologies and stinking of what Eunice later found out was whiskey. She quit drinking when she got the courage to leave her husband, take the girls and start again in California.

"It's okay, Yana. Aunty Yuny is here to take care of you." She embraced her own self as she wrapped her arms around Brianna.

* * *

Eunice sent a text message to Brenda:

> What the hell? Ryan is drunk. Brianna is tired and hasn't
> eaten anything. I'm going to feed her then take her home.

But where was home? To the black and white property in Bukit Timah, where the perfect family who took her in was unravelling before her eyes? To her mother's Victorian in Berkeley and a garden of fragrant herbs?

Ryan waited outside the washroom. He seemed to have sobered up. Standing beneath a vase of cherry blossoms, he reminded Eunice of her first boyfriend in college. Sid used to wait for her under the Tulip Magnolia trees near Bancroft Library. They had the same ease, these young men born into lives of privilege. Unaccustomed to being turned down.

"Hi, Daddy. Aunty Yuny's taking me to Toast Box." Brianna reached for Ryan's hand. He held it, swaying back and forth with her.

Ryan couldn't look Eunice in the eye. "Sorry about earlier."

He knelt before Brianna. "Daddy's going to go find Mummy. We'll pick you up later, okay?"

At Toast Box, Eunice watched Brianna happily slurp her Milo. She took a bite of kaya toast, the golden brown rectangle shattering into delicious shards. Something about the simplicity of freshly toasted bread, warm and fragrant, brought her close to tears. Creamy sugary pandan jam tasted like manna from heaven.

"Aunty Yuni, go like this." Brianna swiped the side of her own cheek.

Eunice Baker-Lim flicked a perfect drop of melted butter back into her mouth. She took another bite of the kaya toast, giving in to the joy of pure unadulterated carby goodness. Sweetness she would no longer deny herself.

About the Author

Vanessa Deza Hangad left the tech world to focus on writing and family life. A Filipina-American who comes from a lineage of artists, she currently lives in Singapore with her husband and their son. Her work has been published in *(m)aganda magazine* (UC Berkeley) and *The Very Inside* (Sister Vision Press). Her stories are included in regional anthologies *Rojak: Stories from the Singapore Writers' Group* and *Tales of Two Cities: Singapore and Hong Kong*. She was a blogger for asianbooksblog.com and has flash fiction published in literarykitchen.com.

CAKE

JING-JING LEE

It was during the first day of the wake, when the hired mourners were wailing and pounding their fists on the floor, that I realised I didn't have to wish my father dead anymore. I remembered standing up and walking by them, past my fiancée, past the wreaths smelling of rot, past his black and white photo, to look in on him. Just to be sure. I could hear his sniff of derision, to mean that I was being ridiculous and I brushed a hand in the air the way I would have done had he been around to see it before leaning over the coffin, resisting the urge to put a finger into his waxy forehead. He looked like he had been buffed and shined, his skin stretching over his cheekbones in a way it never had when he was alive. I was reminded of the slabs of raw meat I'd had to handle in the first few years of my training as a chef before I switched to pastry. Not chicken, I thought. Pork. A little off-colour, but smooth. He would have hated looking like this.

I spent more than a year trying to convince him to go to the doctor. By then, he had misplaced four sets of house keys, a single suede loafer, and once, the car for an entire afternoon. It took him losing himself and getting picked up along the expressway at 2 AM in a patrol car to finally say yes to an appointment.

"You should take better care of your father."

The officer who brought him back home looked like he didn't yet own a razor. He had his hands on his waist, was trying to peer past me into the flat. My feet were aching from having stood up for twelve hours straight and I still smelled of the cinnamon buns that had stayed too long in the oven. I could tell he was looking for a woman – a mother, a wife, a daughter – who would know how to soothe an angry old man. It took everything I had not to slam the door in his face. "Thanks," I said. Afterwards, the taste of the word soured in my mouth so badly I had to spit. When I begged my father again later that morning, he murmured yes and I remember feeling relieved, as if it was all over then, that someone would be able to fix him in a snap.

The doctor, a neurologist recommended to us by Sophie's mother, asked him a series of questions ("What's today's date? Can you tell me where you are? Count backwards from 100 by sevens.") while I held my breath. He faltered at each one and finally turned away to look at the framed certificates on the wall, as if none of this had nothing to do with him. I wondered if my mother would have sat in my chair had she stuck around. I wondered if my father would have been here at all if he hadn't beaten her into running away. When the doctor started talking about brain scans and possible treatments, he stormed out, cracking open the silence of the waiting room. The other patients scarcely looked up. I apologised to the doctor before running out after him and watched him pace while I paid for the consultation, all the while trying to apologise to the receptionist with my eyes. I wouldn't have been at all surprised if he had picked up one of their large money plants and put it through the glass front of the clinic. His hands were still shaking with rage when he brought the car keys out of his pocket.

"So, what? I don't understand. The doctor told him he has Alzheimer's, right?" Sophie said during Sunday brunch, froth bubbling around the corners of her mouth the way it did when she got worked up.

The congregation had spent most of the morning praying for my father. I spent the time thinking about the "special" to put on the menu the following week. Red velvet? I wondered. When they said "amen", I had decided – a berry galette, simple, rustic.

"No," I said, "dementia. He wanted to run some tests before making the diagnosis but Pa just left …"

"I don't understand. That doesn't sound like him at all."

Of course it didn't. In front of her, he was the man in the pro-family poster (albeit a few decades older) carrying his kid on his shoulders.

"I'll speak to him," she said.

I was about to tell her it was no use when she waved the waiter over. "*Har kau*," she started, "congee, *chee cheong fun*, chicken feet, turnip cake."

"Enough, enough," I said.

While I slept off lunch, she made my father a cup of coffee and sat him down for a chat. The clinks of her stirring spoon invaded my dreams. In it, I was at work, watching the new boy stack cup upon cup on the espresso machine, building white porcelain towers along the chrome top. When I woke, it was done. She didn't have to say anything. I knew from the way she was sitting on the sofa, feet kicking back and forth in the air, that she had won.

* * *

"Paul? You okay?" Sophie said. Most of the guests had left, even her parents and siblings. It was just her now, and my relatives, the ones I never spoke to. They were playing a game of mahjong, making a point of clacking the tiles as violently as they could. "Better to ward off any ghosts or cats," an aunt said. All day long I had watched them gather at the back of the funeral tent while my father's friends and his acquaintances from church sat in front, glancing askance at them while they cracked sunflower seeds with their teeth and propped their legs up on their plastic chairs. I looked over at them and saw at once how much my cousins resembled my father, even the women. I wondered when I would see them again, after this was all over. Probably never, I thought.

"You should go home," I said, "it's almost one."

"I'm wide awake. Gracie got me coffee just now and my mum, too. I had four today."

I shrugged. "Okay, can you get the *pek kim* box and count the money in it?"

When I went upstairs to wash my face later on, I saw that she had undressed and fallen asleep on my bed. I heard her waking to the sound of an alarm in the morning. Minutes later, the door to my father's room opened and I imagined her glaring at me lying in my father's recently vacated bed. I could picture her face but not the expression on it and tried not to frown as I went through the various possibilities. Anger? Resentment? Resignation? All three, probably. I lay still until she shut the door with a loud click.

Everyone from the cafe showed up the next day. Boss handed

me one thickly stuffed envelope and several boxes of pastries made by the apprentice. I opened up the box for a look: the fruit tarts were too blond but the almond croissants looked good and might do for breakfast. I tried to pass them around but no one wanted them when there was curry and rice and noodles. My father would have sneered and said, "You and your cupcakes."

The truth was I hated cupcakes and was relieved when the trend died away. People wanted bread now. And French pastry. I was itching to go back to work. Two more days, I thought to myself.

* * *

Sophie offered to move in when my father stopped speaking and eating. I reminded her that the people at church would find it unbecoming.

"And your father. The way he looks at me already, even now. If you move in with me ..." I wasn't lying. The man scarcely acknowledged my existence and I knew, from the way he sat with his body slightly turned away from me, that he wanted me gone.

"We're as good as married," she said, "what's the harm?"

It hit me then, a sucker punch of regret. The ring, pinhead sized and glinting, made me wince each time it caught my eye.

"It's just not the right time."

"But it will never be the right time. Your father's ill now but when he dies it'll be another year before we can ..." She stopped and pinched her lips together. "I'm sorry," she said.

I wasn't. I was thinking about how long I could make my father last just so I could hold her off.

* * *

From start to finish, it took less than four years. As my father received the news, he sank into his chair and his face stilled and clouded over. It was as if the doctor, in giving him the diagnosis, had waved a stop sign – red and glowing – in his path. He took his medication religiously but it seemed he never once thought about fighting it. I hired a live-in maid. Half a dozen maids, one after the other, until I lucked upon one who had experience with dementia patients. Nina stayed with him for three years, sleeping close by, washing him, taking him to the bathroom. She held his hand on walks even when he took to cursing at our neighbours and stripping in full view of the public. When people stared, she would smile. "Uncle is not feeling well," she would say, her voice bright and loud enough for everyone to hear. On Sundays, she sang while she shaved his slow-growing beard and trimmed his eyebrows, the hair around his ears. I like to think that this was the one good thing I managed to do for my father, hiring Nina.

The only person who had anything bad to say about Nina was Sophie's mother. "You be careful. I've heard stories from my friends. They get vulnerable old people to change their wills and give them everything," she whispered.

I had just finished another twelve-hour shift and could not stop myself from snapping, "Who are these friends of yours?" Then I laughed and she stared at me for a beat before joining in, her eyes still wide. She left soon after that, saying goodbye to my father in the same voice she used on her Pekingese. My father didn't even look up, didn't even grunt the way he did sometimes, as if he understood everything but couldn't be bothered to reply –

it was all beyond him now.

Before my father stopped speaking, these were the things he would repeat from time to time:

"Remember your mother? Remember the *jook* I used to make her when she was sick?"

"The will is in my writing desk. In the envelope together with my coin collection."

"Don't lose the girl. Marry her before she finds out she's too good for you."

"When the time comes, don't let me become one of those … vegetables. Take this and …" He would show me, gripping a pillow in his hands and pressing it over his face until I shouted at him to stop.

* * *

A few of my army pals came on the last night of the wake. They had seen the obituary in the papers, they said, and wanted to offer me their condolences in person. I saw Yong Lim at once but held back, talking to everyone else, passing out packets of green tea at the table when they were done paying their respects. When he finally came up to me, I didn't know whether to shake his hand or pull him into a hug and we ended up gripping each other's arms between us.

"I hardly recognised you," Yong Lim said. We had gone through basic military training together, then ended up in the same unit in cadet school. I tried to recall the hours we had spent together but my mind kept leaping to an image of him lying prone on the bunk bed, sketching in his notepad. He had caught the likeness of everyone in our dormitory with a pencil and handed them out one evening as if dispensing graces or talismans. The shy "Y. L." in a corner of the paper. I had kept my drawing in my wallet until afterwards, after everything, and it was years, maybe a decade before it disappeared. I remembered looking for it when I discovered the loss, how I had walked out of the flat, back into the lift and traced my steps all the way to the bus-stop, how the ground had blurred in front of my eyes when I realised I had lost it for good.

"Yah, put on weight. Perks of the job," I said, tapping my stomach.

"No, it's not that." He narrowed his eyes then and continued searching my face. I held his gaze for three counts before looking away. "So you became a chef after all?"

"Yes, no. Pastry chef. I work at this cafe in Tiong Bahru. You know the one?"

He shook his head. "I'm not much of a cake person."

I rolled my eyes, forgetting where I was for a moment. I wanted to tell him that I knew, I remembered. "It's not just cakes … There are savoury breads. Pies too. You should visit sometime."

Sophie appeared at my side just then. She extended an arm and smiled. "I'm Sophie, Paul's fiancée."

It took Yong Lim a second to recover from his surprise, and another before he forced his mouth into a smile. They shook hands and I sat and listened while Yong Lim told her that he was an interior designer, that he had set up shop with his sister six months ago.

"Hardly getting any sleep," he said.

"Oh? Did you hear that, Paul? Maybe we should think about

it. Start our own business."

Our? I thought. "I bake. I don't do money."

Yong Lim laughed.

* * *

Did I tell you that I'm sorry for your loss?

I feel I might have forgotten. Sorry for your loss.

The message came in while I was rooting through my father's writing desk. The chime of my phone made me feel intruded upon. *Rude*, I thought. When I saw that it was Yong Lim, I put everything back into the drawer and switched off the lights before leaving the room. Later that night, I stared at the message in the dark, until the glare of the phone seeped its way behind my lids and I could see his message long after I closed my eyes. I typed out three different replies before deleting each one. In the end, I left it and went to bed. The cremation was early the following day and I had to rise at five, get myself and everything ready before they came for the body.

* * *

Afterwards, Sophie insisted on driving home with me even though I told her she should go and get some sleep – her eyes were red and she had to work the following day. I had just eased out of the parking lot when she leaned over to switch the car radio off.

"I was thinking," she said, "maybe we should just go ahead with the wedding after all. We've been waiting for five years."

"I don't think this is the right time to talk about this," I said, glad that I had a point for once.

"But it's never the right time with you. Your father's death got me thinking. We should just go ahead. Who cares what everyone else thinks."

"It's not about what other people think. I need more time."

Silence. She turned to look out of her window. When she turned back and spoke again, her voice was different. Softer. "It's okay, Paul. I know what you are. But I don't mind. We'll be happy together. I can make you happy."

"I know what you are." My father had said this to me one weekend, years ago. I was blacking my army boots when he stepped into the kitchen with my phone in his hand. *He's found them,* I thought, *the messages from Yong Lim.* For a moment he just stood there, towering over me, and I watched his hand curl into a fist as I tried to find my voice. Finally, I said, "That's my phone. It's private."

He dropped it and it landed on the floor with a clatter. I closed my eyes. I was sure he was going to hit me or put a chair over my head.

"Nothing is private here," he had said, leaving the flat. We didn't talk for a week after that and we never talked about what happened that day, not to each other.

Sophie was gripping my arm, peering into my face. "It's okay," she said, "I still love you."

*   *   *

That evening, when the funeral was all over, I put the engagement ring in my bedside drawer and fell into bed. I couldn't sleep. I got my phone out and read the message from Yong Lim again. An hour later, I was at the cafe, switching on the lights, getting out a saucepan and a stainless steel bowl, rooting around in the walk-in fridge for good ham and cheese. As I piped the dough onto a sheet of baking parchment, I practised telling him, "I know you don't like cake so I made you this." When I had twenty of them, I dampened my thumb and pressed it gently into each cookie. "Thumbprint cookies," I would tell him. "Savoury, not sweet." I would hand them to him in a box and wait for him to open it up. He would take his time, the way he did when given a gift, and I would wait.

About the Author

Born and raised in Singapore, Lee Jing-Jing graduated from Oxford's Creative Writing Master's in 2011 and has since seen her poetry and short stories published in various journals and anthologies. Jing-Jing's novella, *If I Could Tell You*, was published by Marshall Cavendish in 2013 and her debut poetry collection, *And Other Rivers*, was published by Math Paper Press in 2015.

THE VEIL

ALICE CLARK-PLATTS

Barely knowing it, she had arrived. Now seven thousand miles lay between them. The damp zinc-coloured heft of the London skies had gradually given way, through a night and a day, to the weightlessness of this city. Now, the air was a burn of a whisper on her nostrils and her feet were light, lighter than before.

Now, she had escaped.

She followed the line of the Singapore River, walking opposite the sweet-wrapped, jaunty shophouses of Clarke Quay. She leaned against a rail and watched a bumboat idle by, cutting through the water with the accompanying drone of a computer-generated voice of a tour guide. She moved further along the river towards the stately Fullerton Hotel, which swelled through the shimmer like the high white wall of a cruise ship. She thought of warehouses stashing giant crates; coils of rope on decks; tigers prowling in cages below. Raffles himself pointing to land masses, shouting and ordering the coolies around, building great empires.

She felt a spill of excitement as she walked: *that right at that moment, no one knew where she was or what she was doing.* She had no use for Facebook or Twitter anymore. She would not be emailing or calling. She breathed in deeply, swinging her arms beside her like a young girl.

But if they could see her now.

In *Singapore*.

Racing to the airport, scanning the departure boards, no time to think or reflect, her passport hot in her hands, the word had conjured up cool images of palm trees and pineapples, of white sandy beaches. Of refuge and peace.

And now here she was. She smiled as she looked at her feet walking the concrete pavements in Asia. It was going to be a good day.

Soon, she had gone as far as Chinatown. The streets were narrower there, squeezing in on her shoulders, the squat buildings festooned with paper lanterns dangling close above her head. She had to duck and weave to make her way through the tourists who would halt unexpectedly in front of her, magpies waylaid by waving golden cats, by gaudy placemats.

All at once, she didn't like it. She tried to stave it off with a cold glass of Tiger beer which left her palms wet and her head in a fug. And maybe it was because of that, or maybe it was because of the people jolting her path, but the day was no longer good. A tiny rip appeared in its seam and then there was breathlessness, there was leaden apprehension, there was guilt.

She retreated inside a cool, dark building opposite the bar: inhaling softly, gently again, regaining her equilibrium. She was in a small museum, a gloomy hall. She caught sight of herself in the reflection of a glass cabinet inside which were little models of rickshaws with metal spokes in their large wheels like spider's webs. Her face looked back at her in a quizzical fashion, hair springing up in a frizz above her forehead. Turning her head quickly away, she moved further on inside.

The stairs were black and rickety and creaked as her weight landed on them. She touched the walls either side of her, pushing lightly against them as if to test their strength. She emerged into a large space, wooden and sliced as a jigsaw into smaller rooms, where Chinese immigrant mannequins stood frozen in time, rictus grins on their faces.

Staged tables were strewn with Mahjong tiles; a red-painted egg hung from the ceiling above a baby's cot, a cobbler's kiosk was bedecked with metal lasts and a wooden hammer. From hidden speakers came the chatter of a million voices speaking in dialects strange to her, gabbling a stream of secrets hidden from her.

She bent her head into one room where a white veil hung from the window. This was the bride's room: satin slippers were positioned near the wooden bunk, a tiny cracked mirror was propped up above the sink, a red sash lay on a chair. She paused at the threshold, observing it all. Her hands were up at head height, heavy on the door jamb. The babbling voices continued.

A soft breeze moved the edge of the veil across the yellow pane of glass where it was draped. She watched it caress the wooden slats of the shutters, looked at it twisting in the borrowed light of the cubicle. Her veil had been edged with tiny pearls. They had weighted it, fixing the gauze to her head and framing her face. It had felt tight, as she'd moved around the party. She hadn't been able to turn her head, greeting people, wafting kisses through the air like butterflies. She hadn't minded this limitation though. All she had needed was the look he had given her, as she'd walked through the church to him. That look.

Through the shroud of the veil.

She pressed her index finger and thumb together tightly until the blood left her nails. The strange chatter receded and she heard only her breath. For a second – a spasm – she became outside of herself. She was only what she saw, not what she had done. She was enjoined in the molecules of the dusty bridal room. She was the veil, the slippers, the sash. It came upon her as a relief, a sinking into a life that didn't involve her. There was no judgement, no anger, no righteous indignation. The scatter of strange voices seeped into her pores, and when they paused, then the sound of her breath was enough.

She was enough.

She bit her lip and was brought back to herself. At once, she could see again her arms; her hands; the ring. She never should have come here. That brief respite, of being in the bridal room, the cobbler's cubicle, it was nothing but a deceit. The morning had tricked her into forgetting but now the memories returned, gurgling thickly through the rip in the seam of the day.

His head had cracked like an egg, red yolk dripping over the wooden floor in the kitchen. His throat had wrinkled like slept-in cotton sheets when the rope was tightened around it. She had looked down at him after it was done with the buttery moon giving her knowing smile at the window. He lay on his back and after all the anger had gone, and the rage, and the fear, all that was left was love.

And now she was free.

She had turned and left, with nothing more than a purse and a passport. Her memories left behind, she thought, with the pennies in the jar on the window sill.

But she was a fool. The memories had seeped in through the tear. He would never leave her. He was there in the little museum in the middle of Singapore. He was there in the cobbler's hammer and the sash. He was in the voices which whispered, the tourists who crowded, the bitter taste of the beer, her reflection in the window. She had come to the farthest place imaginable. A tropical island, a noodle paradise.

But still he followed.

She scurried from the museum, down the weaving streets of the city, suddenly dark and wearisome, suddenly hostile. Faces peered at her blankly, she could see the judgment in their eyes. She batted them away with her hands like flies, occasionally seeing her reflection in passing windows, striking things in the stilted, heavy air like a madwoman. She tripped on the edge of a storm drain and fell into a group of local women standing under the shade of a veranda, gossiping on a corner. Their mouths zipped closed as they moved back, leaving her standing in the midst of their circle.

A stranger.

Time was on the run now. She could taste panic at the back of her throat. She continued to move, pushing her way out of the circle of women. They watched her go without speaking. She wanted to get back to the hotel, to the air conditioning: where the sterile aroma of disinfectant and lilies reigned like kings, and the stench of rotten fruit and acrid tobacco would be banished. Long forgotten now was the benign vision of sweet-wrappers, a cosy marketplace of spices and woven carpets. Now everything was jagged, it spiked and pushed into her.

Now, the heat was oppressive.

* * *

Now, the heat was oppressive. An August day, told only by the patch of blue seen through the small, high window. There was no air-conditioning anymore, there was no sky. Now, she lay flat on her back and looked at the cracks in the grey ceiling, the air caught with dust, cobwebs in the tiny corners of her cell.

Often she looked back upon that day in Singapore. Her last hours of freedom before she had been apprehended from being *at large*. How she had tasted the air and lived in a moment when she was free. Before she had walked into a dark museum and discovered that life can't be left behind, it can't be abandoned. It attaches itself to you, like a shackle bolted onto a wrist or an ankle, a burden that can never be relieved.

He was tethered to her forever. They could put her in a cell, here in the grey and the dark, far gone from the bright colours of the shophouses and the pungent smell of the durian fruit. But, just as she would always remember those things, so she would always remember him as he loomed above her with a flat hand, raised to bruise her. So she would always remember her last fight back, when she took his life from him.

That was his punishment.

It was also hers.

About the Author

Alice Clark-Platts is a former human rights lawyer who has worked on cases involving Winnie Mandela and the rapper Snoop Dogg. Her debut crime novel, *Bitter Fruits*, was published by Penguin Random House in 2015 and the next in the series featuring DI Erica Martin, *The Taken*, was published in 2016. Alice has won prizes for her fiction and her short stories have been published in various anthologies. She is the founder of The Singapore Writers' Group and lives in Singapore with her husband and two young daughters.

ATM Agony Aunty

Melanie Lee

Dear ATM Agony Aunty,

My name is Shirley Wong Siu Mei, or you can call me Slug like what my friends do. You may not know me, but I know you. Every Monday morning, I draw $200 from you before going to the office. But today is a little different. I was wondering if you could help me with something else as well.

Whenever I take money from you, you always show me a wise quote from someone famous on your screen. I love how that gets me all reflective about life and stuff! I'm wondering if you can actually give me a quote to help with something that's bugging me right now? It's about Danny, my boyfriend.

In the eight years that we've been together, Danny is usually a pretty steady guy: handsome but not that vain, rich but quite down-to-earth, popular but not too egoistic, romantic but also can be funny. I'm very lucky to have a boyfriend like him, because I'm just an ordinary girl.

However, these past few months, he just cannot stop talking about getting married. He keeps asking me to commit to a date sometime next year. I mean, yes, we've been attached for some time but I also feel like we're still young – it's only been a while since we graduated from university. But Danny keeps saying that there's nothing holding us back since money is not an issue. He's from a rich family, has a stable job as an investment banker, and already has several properties under his name. His dad, a cosmetic surgeon, has offered to pay for the whole wedding as well.

I'm usually quite *chin chai*, but this is a big thing which I feel cannot be rushed. Danny's been quite annoyed that I haven't chosen a date yet. Keeps sighing and moping about, asking "Are you sure you really love me?" in a super emo way. I also don't know why he's like that. It's not as if other guys are trying to snatch me away from him.

No one's really giving me any proper advice. My girlfriends just squeal a lot if I mention this to them and cannot understand why I'm holding back. My parents adore Danny and already treat him as part of the family. In fact, my dad wants to bring in a fortune teller to choose an auspicious wedding date if I can't make up my mind.

I really need some perspective from someone who is more third-party and objective, you know? So please, Aunty, please tell me what I should do.

> "We must be willing to let go of the life we have planned, so as to have the life that is waiting for us."
> E.M. Forster

Of course lah! Why didn't I see it that way? I get so wrapped up in planning my ideal life that sometimes, I forget that in the long term, my future *is* with Danny. I don't know why, but I've always had this silly idea in my head that I ought to work for a few years first before considering the grown-up stuff. Argh, now I feel like such a lousy girlfriend. How could I have been so self-absorbed? I'm going to make things up to Danny tonight. Thanks for your advice hor! I'll check back in with you next Monday.

* * *

Dear ATM Agony Aunty,

Hey, it's me again – Shirley. So I took your relationship advice last week and well, things got pretty intense.

So here's what happened:

On Monday, I told Danny that we could fix our wedding date on 5th June next year (my birthday, and also the day we got together). He was so happy and finally, that cute, crinkly smile of his came out. I thought, great, no more sulking.

On Tuesday, he officially proposed to me with a six-carat, emerald cut diamond ring (on a sailboat, with a dramatic sunset as backdrop). We announced our engagement on Facebook and that status update got over 500 Likes! It was quite touching to see so many people happy for us. It made me feel like I had made the right decision.

On Wednesday, Danny got right down to wedding planning mode. He bought every single wedding magazine from Kinokuniya. He even decided that "our" song "Let There Be Love" by Nat King Cole should be what I should walk down the aisle to. I felt a little weird about that, I've always thought that it's best to stick to something classical like "Canon in D", but he seemed so excited so I didn't say anything.

On Thursday, we met up with this lady who is apparently

Singapore's top wedding planner. Like many people who meet us for the first time, she seemed taken aback at our visual incompatibility.

"Soooo ... how did you two meet? You seem so ... sweet," she asked as her eyes darted between Danny and me.

Danny grabbed my hand tightly. "We're childhood sweethearts. I was just a teenager when I fell in love with this girl with the most beautiful soul in the world."

"Awwwwwwwwww ..." went the wedding planner as she placed both hands on her chest. "It's so nice to know such unexpected love stories still exist today."

Danny was going to retort but I squeezed his hand to signal to him to let it go.

However, later, when the wedding planner advised me to start immediately on intensive facial and slimming treatments to prepare for The Big Day, Danny chewed her head off.

"What right do you have to tell my fiancée how she wants to look on her wedding day?"

"Oh Mr Lim, please don't take this the wrong way. This is just part of my standard checklist. I ask every bride that, even the pretty and slim ones! It's all about looking one's best for your special day!"

"Excuse me, what century are you living in? A wedding is a celebration of love and not a beauty pageant. I want you to apologise immediately to my wife-to-be and then I hope we never see you again."

So I guess she's not getting the job. But that's Danny, always standing up for me. All these years together, he has never asked me to dress better, lose weight or put on more make-up. He has always accepted me just as I am, and he has never wavered even though far prettier girls are constantly throwing themselves at him.

On Saturday, we were at his place typing out the invitation list on his laptop when I asked if we should invite his mother. Danny's parents divorced when he was eight, and he has not been in contact with her ever since.

"She's moved on. She doesn't need to know," he said a little too quickly.

"But she's your *mother*. She'd want to be there to see you get married. Maybe you can Google her or something …"

"Keep out of this, Slug."

"Why? Why don't you ever talk about her? Danny, we're going to get married soon. I feel we should …"

"No! She's not part of my family anymore so there's nothing you need to know."

And that's when I got really annoyed. I'd just done the grown-up thing by deciding on a wedding date and there Danny was, still acting like an annoying, secretive teenager.

"Dear, I know your parents' divorce was tough on you. But if you can't even be open about something that was such a major event in your life …"

"Slug, I'm warning you, don't push this."

You know Aunty, I'm usually the non-confrontational type. But this time, I felt this was too important to let go.

"Danny, we're going to be married soon. We shouldn't have secrets."

That really riled him up. We proceeded to get into a horrible argument. He threw his laptop against the wall. I cried. And then,

Danny stomped off and hid in his sailboat. (He stays in Sentosa Cove, so his boat was just parked outside the living room.)

Lourdes, Danny's helper since he was a baby, came over with a box of tissues as I sat at on the sofa alone, trying to calm myself down. As she picked up his battered laptop from the floor, she looked at me mopping up my runny nose and said, "I think I need to show you something."

Lourdes scurried to her room and came back with an old photograph of a bikini-clad lady resembling a young Gong Li with waist-length black hair and huge almond eyes.

"Old ma'am – she gave me this photo of herself before she left. 'In case Danny ever wants to remember me,' she said. But he never did," Lourdes whispered.

"Tell me more."

Lourdes sat next to me and pointed to the photo. "Old ma'am – she's called Linda. She is quite a nice lady, but very restless. Sir was always busy with work and neglect her and Danny. She was always looking sad and sighing, then one day she ran away with a Russian billionaire. Old ma'am didn't even want custody of Danny. She wrote an apology letter to Sir and Danny, saying she needed a new start in life. I heard from other maids of Sir's friends that she is living a luxurious life in Paris now. But don't tell Danny I tell you this. I tell you because you are marrying him soon, and maybe this will help you take care of him."

My heart felt so heavy after hearing this. All I wanted to do was to go over to Danny and give him a long hug. But something held me back. Perhaps I was still angry, perhaps the pain felt too private. I left his place without saying goodbye and we haven't talked since.

I don't know what to do – we've never gone for a day without talking! Should I apologise? Is it wrong to be angry with him about this? Should I expect him to tell me everything? Please Aunty, I need your wisdom.

> "I believe that if you'll just stand up and go,
> life will open up for you."
> Tina Turner

Huh? Stand up and go where? Let me try this again.

> "Every time you are tempted to react in the same old way, ask if you want to be a prisoner of the past or a pioneer of the future."
> Deepak Chopra

Are you actually listening to anything I've been saying in my head silently? Oh forget it, you're just a UOB ATM. I'm going off now.

* * *

Dear ATM Agony Aunty,
Now I know that you were trying to warn me last week. I'm sorry for shutting you out like that.

Last Wednesday, I could no longer stand the three-day cold war with Danny, and so I called him up to apologise. I told him that he didn't have to invite his mother to our wedding, or tell me about her if he was not ready to yet. He accepted my apology in a rather chilly manner, but agreed to meet up on Friday, mostly because we'd already arranged a double date dinner with Danny's best friend, Neil, and his girlfriend, Mei, at Les Amis to celebrate our engagement.

Les Amis was the restaurant that Danny brought me to on our first Valentine's Day date. Neil and Mei were in the same secondary school and junior college together with us – so everything felt really sweet and nostalgic at first. Danny seemed to be in a better mood and ordered a vintage whisky from the year we were born. As they congratulated us, Neil suddenly quipped, "Hey you know what, Slug? You're actually getting prettier. Must be all that lovin' you're getting from Danny boy, huh?"

My heart sank as I saw Danny give a chiselled scowl. As I told you before Aunty, he always gets defensive when people comment on my looks. I usually really appreciate that, but at that moment, I just didn't want him to get upset again.

Mei giggled. "Oh my gawd, Slug, last time, you were so *toot* in school last time with messy hair and huge glasses. Who would have thought you'd be marrying our prom king ten years later? Remember how Danny used to tease you all the time?"

Danny grabbed his whisky glass and emptied it out.

Neil, unaware of the growing tension, continued to reminiscence as he swirled his whisky. "Oh yah, I remember! Danny was the one who came up with your 'Slug' nickname in Sec 1 because he said you had 'slimy skin'. And then he told everybody else in school to call you that as well … and oh oh oh … I also remember, he would imitate the way you walk, what did he say it was like? 'Sliding around like a sexless lump?' Ha hah ha! Eh bro, now I know why you did all that teasing. It's because you were in lurveeeeee with Sluggy-wuggy even way back then huh?"

At this point, Danny broke his whisky glass and it shattered all over the table. And that's when something in me just snapped. I flung my whiskey at Neil's face.

"STOP CALLING ME SLUG! I HAVE A NAME, YOU KNOW!" I yelled, before stomping out of the restaurant, switching off my mobile phone and taking a two-hour walk home to clear my head.

When I reached my flat, Danny was pacing back and forth at the void deck. This was a scene I'd seen hundreds of times – arms across his chest, finger drumming ... in a school uniform, in National Service army fatigues, in a polo shirt and berms, in office wear. He always came before the arranged meeting time. He was always waiting.

In fact, Aunty, did you know that Danny wooed me for one whole year before I agreed to go out with him? It was mostly because I couldn't believe that the school hunk and tormentor during the first two years of my secondary school life would actually be interested in me. But he was. He said I was different from the rest of the girls in school whom he thought were vain and self-absorbed. He told me I was the only one he could truly be himself with, and a few times a week, we would talk over the phone at night till our ears burned and the morning sun peeked through the curtains. We both liked soppy romance movies, old jazz standards, and J.D. Salinger novels. We both felt strongly about poverty and orphans and even did volunteer trips to Cambodia together. Danny was always telling me, "We're the real deal, Slug. We're forever." And then he'd kiss me and I'd feel like our souls were like conjoined twins, even if to the rest of the world, we were worlds apart.

Last Friday though, Danny made no such loving declaration when he saw me approaching. He just shut his eyes tightly as if he had a migraine and asked wearily, "What's going on?"

I took a deep breath and gave him the reply I rehearsed many times during the walk home. "Danny, it's too soon. I'm not ready to get married. And I think these past few days have shown that we have some serious issues to work out."

He combed his fingers through his hair and swore under his breath.

"Slug, what are you talking about? We've been together since we were sixteen. We can complete each other's sentences. My dad and your parents have given us their blessings. I've been ready to marry you since we were teens. But if you still don't think you're ready, then maybe we should reconsider our relationship."

"Danny, please don't give me this ultimatum."

He looked at me incredulously. "What are you trying to say?"

My heart was pounding so hard that my ears throbbed. "Danny, I'm saying that if you really can't wait, then don't."

He grabbed my hands and brought me close to him so that his dark brown eyes could look into mine. "I want to spend the rest of my life with you. Why are you being such a prissy bitch about this? It's not like there are other guys lining up to marry you, you know."

I snatched my hands away from him.

"So I should marry you because no one else would want me?"

That's when it hit me: I've always thought Danny loved me *despite* my lack of good looks, but now, I realised that he loved me *because* I was ugly.

"Slug, you know that's not what I mean ... I love you *exactly* the way you are, I always have ..."

"Maybe that's the problem. You think that me looking like a slug is a guarantee that I will never leave you."

"Slug, shut up! You know our relationship has never been about physical attraction!"

There was a long, uncomfortable pause as I stared at this beautiful man who used to make me feel I was beautiful.

"This is why we won't work," I finally said.

He began shaking his head vehemently. "No. Hell, no. This is not happening. You don't get to break up with me. You, of all women, don't you dare do this!"

He sounded angry but his eyes were full of tears. He already knew what I was going to do next.

I pulled the engagement ring off my finger and dropped it into his shirt pocket.

"Slug!" he cried as I walked away from him.

And the last words I said to Danny were, "My name is Shirley."

I guess this is my very long-winded way of telling you that I broke up with Danny. Can you send something over to comfort me? I never knew heartbreak could be so heavy and painful. Sorry for getting your keyboard wet, Aunty. I'll wipe up with tissue in a bit.

> "Think of all the beauty still left around you
> and stay happy."
> Anne Frank

* * *

Dear ATM Agony Aunty,

Shirley here. You must be wondering how I've been doing. Well, this was probably the worst week of my life. But thanks to your advice, it hasn't been as torturous as I'd imagined.

My parents were really upset about the broken engagement – not because I had lost such a "good catch" like Danny, but because they saw how much I was hurting. They've been cooking up all my favourite dishes and brewing double-boiled herbal soups every evening for "strength". My mum hinted that I should go on a blind date with her friend's friend's doctor son, but I am enjoying their home-cooked food too much to be bothered.

I'd expected my social circle to disappear after breaking up with Danny, but some of our mutual friends still check up on me, including Neil, who came over with an apology bouquet of white orchids. He'd thought he'd caused the break-up after shooting his mouth off at Les Amis. But after I'd told him what had happened, he said, "You know, Slu ... I mean, Shirley, you deserve a guy who appreciates your beauty, both inside and out."

I've been taking early morning walks around my neighbourhood these past few days since I don't sleep much. I realise how much of the world I've not seen after being immersed in Danny's life for so many years.

I've also been talking more to my colleagues, and discovered that three of them have also recently broken up, and we've arranged to go for drinks this Friday to commiserate. I like how they call me "Shirl" in the office.

It will take a while before every small thing stops reminding me of Danny. I heard he's planning to take a year off to travel around the world, so perhaps that physical distance will also help in getting over him. Is it possible though? How does someone ever get over a guy like Danny?

Oh crap, I'm tearing again. I really need something to get me through the week ahead, Aunty. Could you please help?

> "To love oneself is the beginning of a lifelong romance."
> Oscar Wilde

Oh Aunty, I couldn't have said it better myself.

About the Author
Melanie Lee used to daydream about whirlwind romances involving New Kids on the Block. Since then, she has become a little more realistic about love and life, and enjoys writing the occasional dysfunctional short story. Melanie is also the author of *The Adventures of Squirky the Alien*, a children's picture book series, and *Imaginary Friends: 26 Fables for the Kid in Us*, a collection of illustrated short stories.

BAYSHORE WAKE

MARION KLEINSCHMIDT

When Maeve enters the Bayshore condo lobby, ice air washes over her like a blessing.

Five past midday, only late by a sliver. She needs to brave the function room eventually. For now, she focuses on the luxury of the air-con gliding down her neck and into the cinches of her tight, unbreathing dress – her only black dress.

She tries not to think but to let the imprint of the condo grounds linger on her mind. There are the orange arrows of bird of paradise flowers; the black and white fans of mynahs in flight; marvellously intact children in the condo paddling pools, around them mothers and helpers bent over their smartphones.

In the centre of the lobby, the giant sphere of a cactus rests on a black cube of marble and absorbs her attention. There is something comforting in the taut green globe, prick-studded on the outside, all flesh and juice inside. "I THIRST NOT" reads an embossed plaque. How true. Those little woolly cacti they used to have lined up in her childhood house in Dublin – Ma only watered them when she thought of it; they endured, shrouded in a fuzz of needles.

Maeve decides not to remember and clings to her senses instead: the reflection of her frizzy, wheat-blonde bob in the elevator door, the icy edge of the marble slab …

She is about to prod one of the globe's waxy-looking grooves when she feels a hand between her shoulder blades. A familiar bass voice warms the room, "Maeve, you made it – you okay?" She's used to Jezz turning up at the heart of any good party. Right now, he monopolises the epicentre of everybody's grief.

Maeve keeps facing the cactus. She shakes off his hand without turning around. "Is everyone else already in there?"

"Yeah. We're about to watch my tribute to Anabel."

Anabel.

* * *

Now Maeve can no longer un-think her. Cannot un-see the way Anabel skipped across the sweltering saloon lounge. Turning eleven among adults at Punggol Horseback Adventures. Shoulder blades protruding from her camisole like grasshopper wings. Unflappable, yet fragile. Nervous energy crackling about her like static. How with that copper cloud of hair around her impish face she bee-lined straight for Maeve, targeting her with a Hello Kitty comb …

* * *

Gently, Jezz spins Maeve around by the wrist.

She cannot be made to watch Anabel on film. Not today. "Do you have to turn everything into footage?" she croaks. His bloodshot eyes make her regret her words. "Don't say, I know. It's your language of love."

"My fucking language you bet," he gives her one of his Asian bro knuckle thumps that are mostly ironic, but at this moment the gesture comes with perfect credibility. Jezz was the only dad-like creature for Anabel in Singapore after her father "moved on". He looks tense, hunched around the neck. His long black hair that usually hangs loose is tied into a neat pony-tail. And what's with the psychedelic Grateful Dead shirt? An homage to his California roots? It makes his skin look sallow.

"So how's your film stuff coming along?" Maeve probes.

"Same old. Hella-money for the commercial suck-ups. Nobody wants to screen my real shit."

For a moment, they take each other in, hands hanging limp without gestures to go to.

"You sure look – smart," Jezz offers eventually.

"Is this even really happening?" Maeve hears herself say.

"Wasn't in the script alright." He eyes her bulky tote bag. "I'll go in with you. Brought some liquid lunch?"

"Nope. Just came from an audition. Same old, don't ask …"

Jezz prises open the heavy Function Room door; it gives way with a squelch and they face a chair circle of twenty-odd guests engaged in polite conversation, some with their children in tow, all of them in madly coloured outfits.

"Were we supposed to wear black or rainbow?" Maeve asks under her breath while scanning unknown faces. Their glances avoid her, as if they can identify the bad smell of somebody too close to the core of loss.

"Didn't you read the invite?" Jezz hauls the door shut. "For Anabel's sake, we're keeping things nice and bright – to celebrate her life. And for the vid."

The video message.

Another thing she can't do. Maeve seeks refuge in the still life of the snack table: glistening grapes and a pyramid of Chinese barbecued pork strips. She watches Jezz pour Chardonnay into a plastic flute and opens a can of 100PLUS for herself. Out of her tote, she pulls the leopard print pashmina from the audition – dressing up for yet another part.

They grab two empty chairs at the back of the room. Maeve sits down in her wildcat cloud of pink while Jezz faces the gathering.

"Thanks for being here, ya all, for the flowers and stuff," Jezz lifts his hands palms up. "We can't display them here, condo rules. But you'll see them in my place when you do the video. Apartment twelve-o-three – make sure you come up and record your message," his voice grows doughy, "for Valerie – Anabel's Mum. We're half a planet away from the real event in County Wicklow, so I edited a short movie as a tribute." He slumps into himself. Like a shot bull, thinks Maeve. Then it rips out of him: "We oughta be throwing her a birthday party, not a freaking wake!"

A vacuum sucks every sound out of the room – except for the whirring of the air-con. Then, the plasma screen bleeps to life and "Hey Jude" starts playing. A couple of gents in batik shirts hurry down the blinds, switch off the lights. Maeve feels her throat constricting: the screen shows a pre-school Anabel jumping across a bouncy castle to the exact rhythm of Paul McCartney singing, "Remember to let her into your heart."

Jezz sinks into the chair beside Maeve, "How fucked up is this?" Then he drops his head into his hands.

At a loss for other distractions, Maeve begins rubbing the tips of her fingers over the velvety irritation of the chair's seat cover.

"We should be with Val right now," Jezz mumbles into his palms, "you most of all. You knew her from college, right?" he continues unaware of the blade he plunges into Maeve.

"We did Drama & Theatre in Trinity together alright, but that's eons ago. Didn't know where she was at. Then bumped into her at the Formula One last September …" The sweet jolt of Valerie, all cello curves in a champagne-drenched slip. Mane held up by shades at the top of her head. Both of them recently sans the relationship that brought them to Singapore. How effortlessly they careered right back into the eye of the party-storm that used to surge around them.

"Seems like you've been hanging with her and Anabel forever, like they totally adopted you. You'd think this city would be the safest possible place for a young girl."

If she weren't so absorbed with rubbing her hands forwards and backwards beside her thighs, she'd have to shut him up right there. Instead, she lets a few moments pass, then says, "Accidents happen, Jezz, nothing we could have done."

He lifts his head out of his hands. "Not that I blame you. It's awesome that you brought her to that ranch, great spot for a kid. Just – she deserved a lot more from life is all I'm saying."

"She sure did," Maeve's most detached self manages to respond. "We all do." Her fingertips have gone pleasantly numb. She is not going to watch this video. But closing her eyes doesn't help either.

* * *

Because there is Anabel again, flapping the comb against her hand at the pace of a jig. Always rope-skipping, coin-flipping. Jittery-bug, Maeve used to call her. And yet, she was so mock sedate, asking, "Aunty Maeve, kind and fair, would you care to braid my hair?"

When Maeve said yes, Anabel curled into her arms like a kitten. Valerie groaned, "No slave labour before cocktails," from across the table and fanned herself with the bar menu. Electricity was down at the Punggol ranch and generator-driven fans wafted stagnant air about their heads. With the help of the Hello Kitty comb, Maeve turned Anabel's fine strands of hair into tight French braids. When the drinks arrived, Val lifted the cherry off the rim of her glass and plopped it into Maeve's mouth. Then, she placed an elaborately silk-ribboned present in front of Anabel: "Happy birthday, doll, something nice to wear for dinner in town."

"I'm sick of your dinners," Anabel didn't look at her. "And of riding ponies. Aunty Maeve says I'm ready for a real horse."

"I'm afraid it's too soon, doll," Val picked up her cocktail.

"Even my instructor says I'm a natural!"

Valerie just swung her curves and her cocktail over to the saloon's piano and launched into a chamber version of U2's "Elevation".

During the Punggol staycation, Maeve's mission was to help make it up to Anabel for a cancelled trip home to Ireland – Val being on call-back for a movie casting. At first, they all found the mock ranch ridiculous. Then, Anabel discovered her skill at riding and Valerie the saloon piano.

"High, higher than the sun," Val intoned. "You shoot me from a gun."

Anabel watched her mother glassy-eyed, not opening the present by her side. Maeve pulled a pack of playing cards from her pocket and started to shuffle. Teasing Anabel out of her pouty stance took plenty of hairdos, horse-riding lessons as well as prolonged poker nights at the outdoor BBQ pit while Val practiced her script. By the end of the weekend, Anabel couldn't hide her joy at Maeve's attentions or keep a poker face to save her life. You literally saw the fine blonde hair lift on her arms when she got dealt a hot hand.

* * *

Maeve's eyes flutter open. On the plasma screen there are black and white stills of Anabel and Valerie, wrapped in jackets and scarves on a rainy day in what must be the Wicklow Mountains. Jezz watches mesmerised, as if for the first time. In the next still, Valerie's dark curls bunch over her daughter's face as she hugs her from behind, while Anabel sticks her tongue out at the camera.

"Still haven't had any – contact from Val?" Jezz asks between two gulps of wine. Maeve lets her silence answer his question.

"Don't sweat it. We all have our coping strategies." He takes an audible breath. "Now don't take this wrong, but they're re-auditioning Val's part for that thriller. Great bucks, to be shot in Singapore. You should go for it."

"Please, not now," Maeve tries to look like she is watching his footage while focusing on the menthol and musk in Jezz's shaving cream. It's not working.

* * *

Instead, there is the gleaming gold coat of the full-sized mare saddled for Anabel's first sunset ride. How eagerly she crunched her bit, specks of dust rising from her stomping hoofs. From the ranch veranda, Maeve and Val watched the line of riders depart against a leafy, light-fringed mass of sea almonds and palm trees. Anabel stood up in the saddle and turned around to wave to them, all confidence and triumph. At some invisible signal, the troop trotted off towards rock-strewn Punggol Beach, the rain clouds above them both blocking and drinking the honeyed evening light.

Shocked into greed by the gift of twosome time, Maeve and Val ordered a pitcher of Long Island iced tea, which came out quickly and perfectly cold – a miracle. The world lost another edge. Cicadas started their mad thrum and a sea breeze slipped around them like cool silk.

* * *

The snap of opening blinds makes Maeve face the final caption on the screen: "Anabel Sullivan. A voice we loved is silent." After a few seconds, the video jumps to the snapshot of a shrivelled new-born, its mouth wide around an inaudible holler. "Great job, Jezz." – "Very touching" – a few ladies in floral print dresses nod in appreciation. A toddler dashes under the refreshments table and his dad pulls him back out by his ankles.

"Thanks for watching, folks," Jezz mutes the sound, but leaves the image on. "The fact you're all here – is powerful. I'll be ready upstairs with the camera. While you wait to come up, please enjoy the food everyone brought. And feel free to share your favourite memories of Anabel."

"I'll be happy to start." A buxom lady in a lemon cocktail dress rises from her chair while other guests top up their wine glasses and grab finger food.

The lemon lady throws back her head, "What a fresh breath of air this girl was! The first time I met Anabel she had just been made captain of St Margaret's springboard diving team. Did you ever watch her dive?" Knowing smiles play across the faces of her listeners. "Holy Moly, she had her eyes on the game. Like a little cannon ball she'd shoot into the water, outjumped girls twice her size ..."

In fact, Anabel's bird-like body weighed next to nothing. Maeve carried her to bed enough times to know. And right there, Maeve knows she won't be able to "share" Anabel, not like this. The video message will have to be her sole contribution. In one swift move, she puts down her can and lunges out of the Function Room to catch up with Jezz.

* * *

"Did you know I was the first she called after it happened?" he asks her as they wait side by side for the elevator.

"I was there."

"Yeah sure, sorry." He stares down at the wine glass in his hand. "Hey, is it okay to ask – what exactly went down in Punggol? I mean, Val was too shook up to go into the details. She said something about bicycles?"

On auto-pilot, Maeve recounts how the mare was paranoid of bikes and the Geylang cycling club zoomed by that very evening all neon and flashing lights. How the horse went daft, jumped right into one of the bikes and threw Anabel against a tree. Snapped spine, no prolonged suffering. How they saw the horse canter back towards them – riderless.

"Holy shit."

"Mad thing is – the cyclist survived. Just the bike was trashed."

The elevator's doors rumble open and they enter its mirrored interior wordlessly. Maeve steps towards her pale and angular reflection.

She will never un-see Anabel's moon-white face as they rolled her into the ambulance before rushing her to Raffles Hospital – for nothing more than a death certificate. The first and only time Anabel ever made a perfect poker face. Later, when it was all over, Maeve and Val took out one braid after the other until Anabel's hair curled for once just like her mother's.

"Val hasn't taken any of my calls since the accident," Maeve confesses.

"They say this is not a city where you see people die. Expats I mean – we all bury our folk back home, don't we?"

"You think she hates me now?"

"Dang no. You two were like that," he crosses middle over index finger. "Just sometimes when people get hit too hard, it's like they can't speak any more." He grabs his throat and opens his mouth to show the effect. "Not to those who are real close anyways."

"You two were pretty close at one point?" Maeve turns away but stares at Jezz's eyes in the mirror.

"An awesome mistake and no regrets." He holds her gaze. "That was long before you entered the scene. Still adore her.

205

Organising this thing for her is the best I can do now."

"Why would she want my voice on video if she doesn't want it on her phone?"

"That's precisely why. No one will be at the other end. Right?"

*　*　*

The lift boings and releases them onto a windy open-air landing with a view of the tanker-studded Strait. To Maeve, there is something achingly familiar about the scattered toy-sized boats, a view reminiscent of her Changi landings and departures, beginnings and endings. Jezz punches a code to let them into a small, spotless apartment oozing lily and lavender smells. The place chokes with bouquets, pollen dusts the counters.

Val's freckled knuckles as she poured the iced tea. Brown of her eyes, like wet earth after rain, amber flecks making them snake eyes. The sexy, hungry gap in her teeth. How Val had ordered the patio table and chairs under a bottlebrush tree, screened from sight by the drooping, flaming-red branches. How she slid off her shoes and sat cross-legged on the metal chair, the tunes from the saloon mixing with the sting of frying chilli in the air. At the corner of your lips. As the orbit of your hips.

And of course Maeve's dying for a drink. To unhinge her, to take the needle off her mind's broken record and to replace it with the sound of golden liquid splitting cubes of ice.

Sweet cold bit down her throat the moment Val's eyes went bright with curiosity, not dark with refusal. When Maeve took Val's shades off the top of her head. Opened her hair. Put her hand there. Her lips. It came with the urgency of milk bubbling over, her own responsiveness. One more touch. One question mark traced on her thigh: "Would you?"

Maeve fingers the speckled lily petals while Jezz re-positions the camera on its tripod. He fiddles with the cables, taps the mic, tells her to take a seat on the cream leather couch, which is bathed in sunlight from the window beside it. He has this way of bouncing back and forth between gushing intimacy and catatonic absorption. Had Anabel been here often? A Lapu Lapu warrior statue from the Philippines lacks one hand, the wall behind it is covered with blown-up Polaroid shots from Burning Man – bare-breasted girls juggling hula hoops, a Ferris wheel on fire.

Jezz is focusing the camera's unblinking eye on her now. Like an iris, its lens deepens and widens. Already, Maeve feels observed, lacking.

"You ready for this shit?" Jezz doesn't look up.

"Mmmh." Maeve pulls up her feet from the cold marble floor onto the sun-warmed leather.

"You can always send in your own vid later," he goes on.

"It's okay, Jezz, I'm doing it." Her mind gropes for a beginning, a groove.

"You're good to go, Maeve."

A green light flickers beside the lens.

"Okay, I'm on. Wow." Maeve inhales deeply; the conditioned air tastes stale. "Well then, Valerie." She puts her feet back on the ground. "Here we all are, thinking of you. Thinking of Anabel."

"You should talk to Anabel directly, you know," Jezz interrupts.

"What do you mean, talk to her, like pretend she's here?"

"She's right here with us, yeah."

Maeve snorts and starts over.

"Hi Val. This is difficult. It's hard to believe Anabel's gone from us. I needn't tell you about pain," the sound of her own voice makes her gag, "I'm not – fuck this! Jezz. This is insane."

"Oh yeah?" He steps back, a freak tremor has come over him and his voice sounds shrill. "Know what's really insane? If you got nothing better to offer than glossy condolences. Like you're just dumping cream all over Anabel's coffin."

"Says the man who hides behind the camera."

As he steps back to the tripod, his sweaty hands slip on its arm. He wipes them against his psychedelic T-shirt, lowers his voice.

"Keep going, M. I'll cut'n'edit."

Seeing Jezz like this actually calms Maeve down. She waits for her words to come. There is the sound of aeroplanes, the hum of the fridge.

"It was mighty getting to know you, Anabel. On this island in the tropics. Didn't think I'd care so much about a girl I didn't even know existed until last year. And you were right, you're a total natural at so many things. You copped on to more than any of us adults. And you were cool about it all. Loved us back better than we deserved.

Thanks for that.

Right now what I want you to know is that – your mum will always have a home with me. If she says the word, I'll book a flight and come to Ireland. If I hear nothing, I'll keep offering. Simple as that.

Oh, and in case you were wondering – that horse is fine. They were going to put her down but your mum stopped them. I know you cared for that mare. She didn't mean any harm. None of us did.

Now watch this …"

Maeve roots around her slouch bag on the floor, flips open her compact mirror and tilts it into the sidelong rays of tropical sunshine, bouncing them back up against the wall. A small gasp comes from Jezz as he swivels the camera to capture the effect.

"I can't say rest in peace, Anabel, you won't. You exist in everything we see with your eyes." Maeve lets the chink of silver pass over the juggling nudes, handless Lapu Lapu, the colourful cloud banks of bouquets. "I wish I'd had more time to be someone in your life. Still, you're the one with all the power. I guess what I want to ask you is – can you forgive us all this stuff we can't forget?"

Maeve flips the mirror shut, gets up and holds her hands out against the camera, a convict leaving court. She rushes past Jezz into the bathroom with its fancy German taps and marble tiles and sticks her head under the sink. Drinks in long greedy gulps.

On the way to grab her bag, she hears Jezz sniffle.

"I can't do this sort of thing, Jezz, I'm sorry."

"Bet you could use a stiff one now. I know I do."

"No, Jezz – d'you know – I'm off the booze."

"For real?" Jezz starts shutting down the camera.

"I was never really into the booze. More like – into the moment. I didn't do it for her. It won't change what happened. I did it because there's nothing left to drink for."

"Good for you, I guess?" He gives her shoulder a brief, tight squeeze. "You done great here. Make sure you audition, okay?"

"Sure thing."

* * *

The mirrored elevator cube plummets her back down to the ground level. Maeve lets her hand trail the cool glass door to the Function Room whence laughter bursts, the clinking of glasses, amused shrieks of children – but she doesn't open it.

And there it is again. The prickly orb of the cactus, gleaming self-satisfied and taut in the lobby. Maeve is alone with it now. She stalls before facing the muggy embrace of the tropics again. She touches the deep waxy grooves between the spikes with both hands.

It doesn't yield. It's made of plastic.

About the Author

Marion Kleinschmidt was born in Bavaria, educated in Ireland and is a citizen of the world. Her short fiction has been published in Germany (Bella Triste) and Singapore (Ethos Books). She holds a Master's degree in Comparative Literature and feels passionate about creative language in the encounter between cultures, art forms and modes of life. Her online poetry and fiction writing workshops at www.coill.net provide an equally diverse space for writers from around the globe, embodying Marion's belief in the power of writing in excellent company.

MERLION'S MAGIC

S. MICKEY LIN

Sarah grabs her yellow Hermès bag to head out of the Wealth Capital Management office. Elisa, her younger, sinewy colleague, stops her with an impish chuckle.

"Tonight's going to be epic, Sarah. Make sure to remember every single detail."

"Did I forget about a major function?" Sarah pulls out her cell phone to check. It is 6 PM and her calendar is empty.

Elisa elbows her playfully. "Let's just say, Keh called to ask for my opinion about your ring size, your favourite music, and stuff like that. If I didn't know any better, I think he's going to propose. He specifically asked me about your availability for tonight." Laughing out loud, she adds, "But you didn't hear from me."

Sarah thanks Elisa and quickly exits the office. In the high-speed elevator, she catches her own reflection in the stainless steel door. Her attempt at suppressing her grin only makes the apples of her cheeks ripen and push against her brassy blonde, shoulder-length hair. She eyes her ring finger, her mind swirling over the possibilities.

Keh, her boyfriend, is finally going to pop the big question. Sarah remembers when she first ran into Keh Lin at Shakespeare in the Park at Fort Canning. It was the opening night of *The Tempest*, her favourite Shakespearean play. They just happened to sit next to each other. She noticed his soft, cinnamon eyes and strong chin and he noticed her glance. He started to recite Shakespeare's Sonnet 50 as a way of striking up a conversation. They finished the sonnet in unison and he asked her out on a date. They have been together ever since.

The elevator reaches the ground floor and Sarah exits Asia Square Tower. The wretched humidity assaults her immediately. She can feel faint perspiration forming on her upper back. A native of Portland, Oregon, Sarah is accustomed to gentle breeze with a pinch of grassy pollen in the air. Only being with Keh made the humidity slightly more tolerable. He is the singular reason she puts up with her daily battle against sweaty stickiness.

She strides over to the bus stop in front of the Ogilvy Centre. Unlike the modern sleekness of Asia Square Tower, the stately building with its decorative marble columns and cast-iron balustrades bespoke of a bygone era in Singapore. Although the nation is less than sixty years old, some of the city's buildings are much older and remind Sarah of its rich history. Unfortunately, the short five-minute walk has completely drenched the back of her silk blouse and Sarah is in no mood for such appreciation.

Sarah boards Bus No. 196. It is brimming with executives heading to their next appointments. More weary passengers board behind her and she is pushed to the back and against a window. Squashed and clammy, she dreams of Keh's proposal as a form of escape. Thinking back, she thought it was strange that Keh insisted on having dinner at home and told her that he would be picking up wine and cheese.

Sarah looks out the window and the sparkling white, twenty-eight-foot-tall Merlion statue appears in the distance. The bus is passing Merlion Park and Sarah sees throngs of tourists snapping selfies in front of the abomination. This fleeting exchange with the Merlion is the worst part of her daily commute. Sarah despises the half-fish, half-lion marble sculpture for the continuous stream of water that gushes from its mouth seems to mock her with its promise to cool the country.

Thirty minutes later, she alights at the Parkway Parade bus stop and makes her way to Marine Green, the prestigious development by Kentwood. Although she may loathe the country, she absolutely loves her apartment. Its distance from her workplace serves as a respite. When she reaches the condo, she takes the lift to the twenty-fourth floor and unlocks the door to her haven – a luxury one-bedroom unit with a grand view of the greenery at East Coast Park and its shoreline.

She closes the door, puts down her belongings, and turns on her 70" TV. The channel opens to the Singapore Badminton Open. It is a riveting game between Singapore and China. She respects how this small country tries to break out of its weight class, but her admiration is constrained by proximity. Sarah is certain that she will admire Singapore even more the further away she is from it. She hears keys rattling outside and turns off the TV. Keh enters with a bouquet of fresh, pink roses and a bottle of the 2003 Domaine Leflaive Puligny-Montrachet, her favourite white wine.

"I thought you were going to bring back dinner?"

"I figure we can go out and eat after a glass of this."

He holds up the bottle to give her a good look at the

Montrachet Grand Cru vineyard emblem. The wine is about $6000 and Sarah knows with certainty that today marks a special occasion. He puts the roses on top of the kitchen table and pours the Montrachet into two Viognier wine glasses. He leaves the wine glasses on the table. He is sweating in his suit and Sarah can tell he's anxious. Unlike her, Keh sweats only when he is nervous.

"Sarah, I have something to ask you."

She gives him an encouraging look, trying to reassure him. "What do you want to ask me?"

Keh kneels down on one knee and pulls out a red signature Cartier box from his pocket. He opens it and she sees a platinum ring with a glittering two-carat diamond in the middle.

"Sarah Lynn Jackson, will you marry me?"

Tears stream down Sarah's face.

"Are you crying because the answer is no?"

"No, silly, I'm crying because I'm happy. Of course I'll marry you."

He puts the ring on her finger and they kiss. Sarah feels as though she is floating.

Keh then takes out two tickets from his blazer's inner right pocket.

"I also got us tickets to the Alexander Pritt concert. I confirmed with Elisa that he's your favourite pianist."

"Oh my god! These concert tickets were impossible to get! I love you, Keh." She kisses him again. "But more than concert tickets, I'd rather get plane tickets. Let's leave Singapore for good. We can go anywhere – Paris, New York, London, or Portland? Anywhere but here."

Keh pulls away from her.

"I know you still have your grandmother here, but we can visit or take her with us. Please, I really can't stand it here," she urges.

Keh looks genuinely torn. "I want to leave too."

"Great! I can start packing and we can be out by next week."

"No, Sarah, you misunderstand. I want to leave, but I can't."

"What do you mean you can't?"

"Listen, I can't leave Singapore because of history."

"Of history? Our relationship is going to be history if you don't tell me what you're talking about. Pride? Your grandmother?"

"I'll tell you the real reason why I can't leave, but you need to give me five minutes. You might think I'm crazy if you stop me halfway."

"Fine. You have five minutes." Sarah takes a sip of her wine.

"How well do you know Singapore's history?"

"The basics. 1965 independence and all that."

"That's a good start. Do you know why it's called Singapore?"

Sarah is annoyed. "Can you just get to the point? I really don't need a history lesson right now, Keh."

"Singapore means Lion City. It's a Malay word. The reason it's called Lion City is because Sang Nila Utama supposedly saw a lion, but that's a myth."

"And what does this myth have to do with you being unable to leave Singapore?"

"Well, the reason it's a myth is because Sang Nila Utama didn't really see a lion. You see, there was never an actual lion." As if revealing the biggest secret in the world, Keh adds, "He saw Merlin."

Keh peers at Sarah to make sure that what he just said

215

registers.

"Merlin? As in the wizard from King Arthur's legend?" Sarah asks again, unsure if the alcohol has affected her.

"Yes! Exactly!"

Sarah's head is spinning. She knows that Keh is a bit eccentric, but has she fallen in love with a buffoon?

"See, I know that you were going to think that I'm crazy. That's why I wanted five minutes."

Sarah looks at her watch. Since she has put up with two years of scorching humidity to find out that the love of her life is loony, she might as well find out just how truly delirious he is. "You have two minutes left," she warns. Then she takes another sip, praying the alcohol will do its wonder soon.

"Don't you find it strange that Singapore is the only developed island nation to be perfectly insulated from all forms of natural disaster? Look at Japan with its earthquakes, Taiwan with its typhoons, and Indonesia with its tsunamis."

Sarah frowns. There is some truth in Keh's point.

"You see, it's all because of Merlin. He cast a magical spell that protects the island. But he didn't want people to know that he was here, so he transformed himself into an animal."

"What does this have to do with anything?"

"Sang Nila Utama caught him by surprise, when he was in the midst of transforming from a fish to a lion. He was surprised to see the lion but he was even more surprised when it talked. It told him that its name was Merlin. But Sang Nila Utama, misheard it and called it Merlion."

"And what's your role in all this?"

"Merlin is my great-great-great-great-great-to the thirtieth-grandfather. His spell is such that his bloodlines need to stay in Singapore in order to prevent calamity from happening to the island."

Keh pulls out two passports, one current and one punched through with one hole, from the inner pocket of his suit and opens them to the visa pages. "You see, every time I leave Singapore, a disaster happens. SARS, the collapse of the Nicoll Highway, and the recent stints of bad haze. If you look at the date of the stamps, everything matches up perfectly."

Sarah picks up and fingers through both passports. The dates do seem to roughly fit what Keh is saying. But if she believes his crazy story, then she is stuck in this hellhole.

"Do you have any proof for any of this? I've never seen you do any magic tricks."

"My blood is heavily diluted and no one remembers how to do any magic."

"Great. So you have no proof of this." She takes a huge gulp of the wine.

"I have no proof, but just hear me out. You know the street, Pennefather? You know that King Arthur was King Arthur of Pendragon. Pendragon means Dragon of Pen, the land where he was from. King Arthur came here with Merlin, but it would have been too obvious to call the street Pendragon, so instead they changed it to Pennefather, to signify that he's the father of Pen."

"King Arthur? First Merlin, now King Arthur?! What are you saying? That Singapore is the mythical island of Avalon?"

"That's exactly what I'm saying."

"You almost got me, Keh. You and your fanciful reason for not leaving Singapore, but now I know you're lying. Avalon is next to Great Britain!"

"How do you know that? When King Arthur was injured, he was put on a boat to Avalon. Merlin cast a transportation spell and they ended here, in Singapore."

"That's very difficult to believe."

"It's easy to believe in a wizard who can cast magical spells, but it's difficult to believe that he conjured a teleportation spell? Now who's being ridiculous?"

"This is crazy! We're arguing about fictional people! You just don't want to leave Singapore!"

"That's not true. I would love to leave this place," Keh says with much conviction. "But I can't. My parents are no longer around and I'm the only child. If I leave, Singapore will suffer."

Tears roll down Sarah's face once more. "I knew you didn't love me, but I didn't know it was to this extent. You're lying about the Merlion story. That stupid, ugly excuse for a creature was created in the 1960s by the Tourism Board to attract tourists. The story isn't even real."

"It is real. No one ever talks about how the designer came up with the Merlion concept. He came up with it after hearing about the local legend. A local legend that originated from my family."

"But Merlion isn't called "Merlion" in Malay, is it?"

"That's why I said it's all a terrible misunderstanding. There never was a Merlion, only Merlin. It's all a linguistic misunderstanding. Think about it, the difference is only one letter. Plus, no one has ever found the mythical island of Avalon. It's because they've been searching in the wrong region."

Sarah remains unconvinced.

"Just think about it. Avalon is described as an island blessed in the abundance of fruits. We have a Lychee Avenue, a Cedar Avenue, a Mulberry Avenue, an Angsana Avenue, and a Rambutan Road. If we include Malaysian and Indonesian words, there is Lorong Nangka, Mangis Road, Rambai Road, Duku Road, Chiku Road, Langsat Road, Kenanga Avenue, and Belimbing Avenue. There's plenty more if you want to hear. Also, we have a street called Pennefather. Why would we have a street call Pennefather? Who is the father of Penn?"

"Pennefather is a fairly common last name. That doesn't prove anything, Keh."

"What about the fact that there is only a one letter difference between Merlion and Merlin?"

"Just a coincidence. Many words have one letter difference. Sing. Sting. String. Staring. Starting. The list goes on."

Keh opens his passport again. "My passports and how Singapore gets into trouble whenever I'm not around. Just another random coincidence? Every single time I'm not here, something bad happens. Explain that."

Sarah examines the two passports. This is the hardest one to disprove. "Fine. Let's check it out." She turns on her laptop and types in the dates on his passport.

March 1, 2003 – July 16, 2003. SARS outbreak in Singapore.
April 20, 2004 – April 23, 2004. The collapse of Nicoll Highway and the termination of the rescue efforts.
June 13, 2013 – June 30, 2013. The haze in Singapore.

By all accounts, everything lines up perfectly.

"So? You have an answer for that?" Keh asks.

"Not at the moment. This seems to be more than just coincidences."

Keh smiles. "It is more than coincidences. It's *magic*." He says "magic" like a kid in at an amusement park, bursting with excitement.

"Have you ever tried to exploit it? You know, tell people that they need you otherwise the island's in trouble." Sarah imagines the amount of money that they will be able to generate from doing nothing.

"If I did that, then people who want to do terrible things to Singapore will want to get rid of me."

The thought has not occurred to Sarah.

"What happens if you die?"

"That'll be the end of the island, I think. The spell is such that our bloodline needs to be on the island. Without our bloodline, then the spell is worthless."

"So you can't ever leave Singapore?"

"Not even if I want to. Look at what happen during my NS training in 2003. SARS hit when I was training abroad. I came back in July and it was eradicated." Keh sees the sadness in Sarah's eyes and continues, "I can still take trips here and there, but I can't go away for too long."

"You're basically telling me that we have to live in Singapore if we want to be together."

"What you want me to do, Sarah? I can't just ignore my people."

"Why didn't you tell me earlier?"

"Because I didn't know that I was going to fall in love with you. Then, I was worried that you would think I'm crazy and leave me. I can't imagine a life without you."

"But I absolutely hate it here."

"I know. I know the humidity drives you crazy. I know that you think the people here speak funny. I know that. Still, I'm asking you to stay. For me. For them." Keh points out the window to the passers-by below on the street.

Sarah looks out the window. She sees the ships near the shoreline. She sees athletes running along the park connector lane at East Coast Park. She sees the lush greenery and she thinks of Portland. The cool, fresh air. The snowy nights and snuggling under a blanket while nursing a cup of soothing hot chocolate. An impossible experience in Singapore.

"I need some time to think about this." She downs the last remaining gulp of wine.

Keh locks eyes with Sarah and says, "With the help of your good hands: Gentle breath of yours my sails must fill, or else my project fails, which was to please. Now I want spirits to enforce, art to enchant, and my ending is despair, unless I be relieved by prayer, which pierces so that it assaults mercy itself and frees all faults. As you from crimes would pardoned be, let your indulgence set me free."

"Really? You're quoting Shakespeare at this time? The ending of *The Tempest* at that? Is this some kind of joke to you?"

"Of course not. But just like Prospero in *The Tempest*, I'm truly at your mercy. Magic would be meaningless without you. And know this, I'll do everything I can to make you the happiest woman in the world."

Keh hugs her tightly and Sarah feels her perspiration

S. MICKEY LIN

evaporating. It's intoxicating. Perhaps it's the magic in his blood. She keeps the thought to herself and holds firmly on to him.

* * *

"Did she buy it?" Lewis Ng, a man with shifty eyes, a flat nose, and an unmemorable face, asks Keh. They sit on a shady bench at East Coast Park.

Keh looks around to make sure they're alone. "Unbelievably, she did." He hands Lewis the fake passports.

Lewis laughs at the guilt washing over Keh's face. "Don't worry, she'll get over it." Lewis pockets the passports and hands him a bottle of Tiger Beer.

Keh takes the bottle. "How do you know? She might leave when she finds out the truth."

"You think you're the first person I told about the Merlion's 'magic'?" Lewis lets out a boisterous laugh. "There are plenty of women out there who believed that they're married to the great-great-grandkid of Merlin. It's hilarious."

"That's awful, Lewis. I only did it because I wanted Sarah to stay and I didn't want to leave Singapore."

"What's so great about her anyway? She doesn't even like our country."

"She loves Shakespeare."

"And? His stories are just like these passports."

"It's like what Northrop Frye wrote, 'One uses Macbeth, not to learn about the history of Scotland, but to learn what a man feels like after he's gained a kingdom and lost his soul.'"

Lewis gives him a quizzical stare.

222

Keh continues, "Basically, it doesn't matter that his stories aren't real, what matters is that we get to know how it feels."

"So what does it feel like? To lie to a woman you love because you don't want to lose her?"

Remorse cloaks Keh's face.

Lewis laughs again. "You're so fun to mess with. Relax, man. Every guy has his reason. But don't worry, she'll forgive you. They all do ... eventually."

"How do you know that?"

"You know all this talk about magic? It's really just love. That's the greatest magic in the world. She loves you and so she's staying. She just needed a crazy enough reason to convince herself. If she didn't love you, no matter how ridiculous your story is, she wouldn't stay. It's that simple."

Keh nods in agreement. Lewis may be an unreliable philanderer but he is a master when it comes to reading people. Keh takes a refreshing sip of his beer, satisfied at the magic he has acquired.

About the Author

S. Mickey Lin is a former Annenberg Fellow and graduate of the University of Southern California School of Cinematic Arts. His writings have been published in Hong Kong, Singapore, and the US. He co-edited *Tales of Two Cities*, an anthology of short stories. His short story collection *Uncanny Valley* is published by Marshall Cavendish. For additional information, please check out www.mickeylin.com or follow him at @mickeylin.

COPYRIGHT NOTICES